Aliens We

Ron Mueller

Aliens We

<u>Books and Stories by Ron Mueller</u>

The Door Series
The Door
Aliens We

<u>The Taelo Series</u>
Taelo: The Early Years
Taelo: The Golden Feather
Taelo: Journey of Discovery
Taelo: Dangerous Passage
Taelo: Condor Clan Slingers
Taelo: Circumvention
Taelo: The Journey of Sages
Taelo: Collection
Taelo: Future Leaders Journey

<u>A Taelo Story:</u>
White Swan and Quiet Pheasant
The Child's Name
Floating Cloud
Quiet Rabbit
Busy Bee
Little Otter & Talking Wren
Broken Spear
Burley Bear & Meadow Flower
A Taelo Story Collection

<u>Science Fiction</u>
The Savitar Series:
Journey's End
Savitar
Confluence
Savitar Collection

Bram Nielson Series
The Fold
The Message
Fold Wormhole
Negative Fold
Ripples in Time
Bram Nielson Collection

<u>Single Science Fiction Books:</u>
Current Past and Future
The Event
Viajante 7

Ron Mueller

Aliens We
By: *Ron Mueller*

Around the World Publishing LLC
4914 Cooper Road Suite 144
Cincinnati, Ohio 45242-9998

This story is a work of fiction. Names, characters, places, and incidents either are products of the author's imagination or are used fictitiously. Any resemblance to actual events or locales or persons, living or dead, is entirely coincidental.

Aliens We: © 2024

All rights reserved, including the right of reproduction, in whole or in part in any form.

ISBN 13: 978-1-68223-940-7
ISBN 10: 1-68223-940-3

Distributed by Ingram
Cover Picture by: Artsiom P @ShutterStock

Cover Design by: Ron Mueller

Ron Mueller

Aliens We

Table of Content

Ron Mueller

1

<u>Beyond the Door</u>

The success of the transport Doors had opened up the solar system. Tom and Linda along with their pet mouse had transported themselves from Door to Door; to the Moon, to Mars and beyond. They along with the Door deployment team set up a rotating schedule for a crew of two that continued to deliver the Doors to each of the planets. The ability to transport a human from Door to Door was kept a tightly held US secret. It was this capability that vaulted the US and a few partner countries into an enviable scientific and future economic position.

Tom commented that the Door team would have a life time of work in delivering the Doors. Though Doorship One was destined to deliver ten Doors out beyond the solar system, he wondered if the delivery of those Doors would enable humans to ever penetrate the vastness of the universe. Their delivery would take too long and barely penetrate the vast expanse beyond Earth's solar system.

1 Beyond the Door

He and Linda talked for hours about the limitation of needing a receiving Door to which a person could be transmitted. He made the point that though the solar system would be easy to populate with numerous Doors, the universe represented an overwhelming obstacle since the time to deliver a Door was limited by the speed at which each Doorship traveled and that was like a snail trying to cross a ten lane super highway.

Linda gave a small laugh and said that meant that they had to come up with a better way of travel than was currently available. She preferred to think about riding in an exclusively luxury car and savoring and enjoying every moment to its fullest.

Tom looked at her and said that what was needed was a way to create an opening between the solar system and any point in the universe that could be traversed even faster than her luxury car. It needed to be an opening that allowed a ship to leave the solar system and go through the opening to any point in the universe.

Linda looked at him and asked what he meant by opening a path to any point in the universe. Was that like having a Chunnel from England to France that took no time to transit?

Tom held up a flash light, pointed it at the wall where it lit up a large round spot. He slowly adjusted it and narrowed it to a small bright spot. He then commented that he had just pulled the fabric of space to a point where he could fly from his current spot in space through the hole he had created.

Linda laughed, put her finger on the wall in the spot created by the flashlight and asked how he was going to create such an opening to some distant point in the universe.

Tom shook his head, smiled, and replied that he was counting on her doing that while he figured out where in the universe he wanted to go.

"And how do you suggest I create the opening in the fabric of space.

Tom smiled and said that she was the one that was so good at sewing and cutting fabric to make the many outfits that she had made for the two of them. She should know how to handle the fabric of space.

Linda was silent as she thought about the challenge that Tom was throwing in front of her. She knew that he was serious about figuring out how to bypass the limitation of not only the current speed of the rockets that they had launched but also of the speed of light itself. Since getting to the speed of light was prohibitive making a hole that opened with zero distance to some distant special location bypassed the speed of light.

She walked over to Tom and gave him a kiss on his forehead and told him that she would have to think about his challenge. It was something even tougher than what they had tackled in creating the Door. They had achieved that ability that could transmit humans from transmitter to receiver at the speed of light perhaps they could make the next break through.

1 Beyond the Door

Tom nodded and said that the challenge was to open a Hole with zero distance that led to a desired location in the universe and then be able to transport a spaceship into that universe.

He then asked if such a point might already existed in the form of a blackhole. Could there be natural or organic holes in the fabric of space?

Linda shook her head and commented that she had no idea and she was not going to attempt to travel to one or into one. She pointed out that the closest blackhole was well beyond the distance that they could send a rocket and expect to get there within their lifetimes.

Tom nodded and said that he was not thinking about going to a black hole but about the fact that the math associated with a black hole might bet the clue in how to create the opening to far of galaxies.

Linda sat down beside him, put her hand on his and asked him if he had a clue as to the complexity of the physics and mathematics associated with the activity of a blackhole.

Tom nodded and suggested they call together the Door delivery team and share their desire to open a way to distant galaxies and see if they could come up with a clue on how to get started.

Linda shook her head and suggested that they first discuss this with General Martinez to see if there was any interest in setting up a team focused on opening the way across the galaxy. She pointed out that such an effort could be helped by being funded so that the two of them would not once again create a personal financial hole.

Tom nodded and said that he agreed with her approach but suggested they also connect with the rest of the Door team members to see what their interest might be in participating is such a venture.

It was very early in England when Tom made his call to General Martinez who was enjoying a steak dinner with his good friend General Delaney. The General realized that it was very early in England and asked what Tom was doing up.

Tom let him know that he and Linda were having an early morning cup of tea and a scone, had been discussing opening the door to the rest of the universe and had decided to see if he had any interest in financially backing such an effort.

The general was silent for a moment. He asked if Tom had come up with another break through.

Tom admitted that so far he and Linda had only discussed such a break through at a superficial level but had several ideas of how to make the break through happen.

General Martinez answered that he needed to see if the President was interested in expanding the Door Project Charter to include funding this new idea. He replied that he was interested and would follow up to see if the current program could be expanded to fund a new break through idea.

When he hung up he looked over to General Delaney and commented that his two wizard scientists were contemplating a new way to travel through space that would make his space force look antiquated.

1 Beyond the Door

General Delaney shook his head and replied that he was beginning to feel really old. His space ships were being negated as they sat enjoying their evening dinner as the door modules got delivered through the solar system. He figured that travel beyond the solar system would need to be based on something more sophisticated than the current Doorships but he had no idea of what that technology might be. He chuckled and said that he also had no idea how the current Door process worked even though he had transported to Door Ship One and back several times. The only thing he knew was that he felt better at this point in his life then he had ever felt before.

General Martinez sat quietly as he chewed on the steak that had been sent to him by Joe's father. He looked over to his friend and said that they should go visit Joe while he and Lydia were both at the ranch and discuss it with them. Joe was the reason that the door program had survived several sabotage efforts and Lydia was the person who had set up the rotating delivery team that the two of them were a part of. If they thought Tom had a good idea he would take the next step and get the President into the discussion about funding another breakthrough.

The Door delivery effort had become a total team effort. Lydia had figured out that everyone could participate by taking turns being the crew on the delivery space ship on a monthly rotation basis. This allowed each of them to spend time on Earth while the years of delivering the Doors throughout the solar system took place.

It averted having to spend countless years in space and it allowed each of the team members to let their bodies rejuvenate since they were able to limit their space time to two months a year. She had jokingly commented that it was the ultimate in having work-life balance which in their case was space-life balance.

She and Joe were enjoying their home life by having taken up residence at Joe's father's ranch. They had decided that living on the ranch allowed them the chance to ride, develop their archery and shooting skills and enjoy the beauty of the land.

Joe had laughed and added that he liked the idea because there was a work crew that did all the work on the ranch.

Uncle Ted and Trey were very happy to have the two choose to live on the ranch. Trey commented that there was plenty of room in the house and he enjoyed taking walks with Lydia and talking with her.

The call from Jorge as they usually referred to the General, surprised them. He asked if he could come to the ranch to discuss a new direction the Door program might take.

Joe was quick to reply that Jorge did not need an excuse to come to the ranch to enjoy one of Uncle Ted's delicious meals. He then asked when he would arrive.

Jorge laughed as he replied that he and General Delaney were in a car stopped at the end of the ranch driveway.

Joe's dad was sitting on the porch with the two of them listening to the call. He chuckled and said the two of them should drive the rest of the way in. He added that they had a couple of beds in the bunk house and after the two cleaned a couple of horse stalls the beds were theirs for the night.

Jorge laughed again and said that he would drive up to the house but he was not sure that the two of them were skilled enough to do the work to earn the use of the bunk house beds.

Uncle Ted greeted the two and joked that he had talked to the leader of the ranch work crew and had been told that they did not want two green horns messing with their horse stalls. He added that they were lucky to arrive early enough for him to modify his dinner menu by adding more water to the gruel he was preparing.

After everyone got done giving and getting hugs, Joe asked why the two of them had chosen to drive to the ranch for the discussion.

Jorge smiled and jokingly replied that he had come for Uncle Ted's gruel. Then he shared the call he had received from Tom and Linda.

Lydia replied that she was undoubtedly biased but she would support any idea that the two of them had.

Joe shook his head and added that neither he or Lydia could be objective about their answer since it was Tom and Linda's Door break through that had given them both a chance for a long life after having been given death sentences for their cancers.

Jorge nodded and said he had the same problem since they were also responsible for saving his career. He had really come to hear exactly what the two of them had said. He felt that his bias should not be the reason to ask the President to fund this new idea.

Lydia nodded and then suggested that he share Tom and Linda's idea with the President and ask her what she thought should be done about it. Let the President decide how to handle it. Let her do her job. She felt sure the President would be in support and she had the means to free up any money it might take.

Gerald smiled and said that her words were exactly the ones that he would listen to and that Jorge should follow.

2 Only If

2

<u>Only If</u>

It had been almost two years since the Presidential election. President Lacey McAdam had benefitted greatly by the landslide victory. The words Joe had used to support her run for President as Doorship One began its journey had left her competitor in the dust and made her coat tail extra-long.

She was happy that she had been one of the person's that had officiated at his wedding and pronounced he and Lydia, husband, and wife. That had given her one opportunity to show her support and appreciation for the two.

The heroic actions he had taken to overcome a near death and a sure disaster had kept her and everyone in the White House situation room at the edge of their seats. They were all yelling in celebration as Joe took control and manually launched the module that all of his team were in and managed to make a successful escape as a missile blew the booster rocket into bits.

Then his successful transition to the Doorship module using fire extinguishers as booster jets and flying across the length of a football field to the spaceship module kept everyone in the situation room silent until he entered the module. It was a moment that seemed to be touched with magic.

It was also at that moment that she had given the order to eliminate all the missile launch sites in the areas held by ISIS from where the attacking missile had originated.

Her actions and the amazing twenty point boost that Joe Elsinger's endorsement made as he and Doorship One left the orbit of Earth gave her a landslide victory that that gave her party control of both the House and the Senate.

When General Martinez called and asked if he could have a moment of her time in person, she had asked how much money was he after but had immediately let her secretary know that she was meeting with the General at the time he requested.

She was now sitting across from him as he quietly shared the fact that before bringing a special request to her, he had stopped by the Elsinger ranch to discuss this with Joe and Lydia. He had sought their consul since the two were direct beneficiaries of the last time the President had funded a significant breakthrough and it had changed their lives.

Lacey smiled, said that he didn't need to back up his request by referencing Joe and Lydia and she knew that he had really gone to the ranch to enjoy Uncle Ted's cuisine.

Jorge laughed and said that was true but he had gone there because Tom and Linda were making the request for funding to support their new breakthrough goal of creating a way to leap instantly from the solar system to any point in the Universe.

Lacey shook her head and asked whether he thought that would ever be possible.

Jorge looked at the President and replied that when she had given him his current assignment he did not believe that transporting a person instantly from one location to another would ever be possible in his life time but now he had personally transported out to Doorship One, spent a month there each time and had transported back two times.

So, did he believe in Linda's and Tom's new breakthrough goal? He said that he was just as clueless as he had been about their previous one.

Lacey was quiet as she thought about the positive power that the US now exerted based on deploying the Door technology that not only transported a person across millions of miles but it also cured most illnesses when doing so.

The US was now in the process of doing a worldwide deployment of the Door technology as cancer curing units. It was slowly becoming clear that the transport process cured all diseases. She was also aware that only a few countries knew about the delivery of the Doors throughout the solar system.

She had been wondering how she could position Craig Lebak, her current vise president so that the vision that she and he shared could continue for the near future. What she now envisioned was a breakthrough that would coincide with the timing for the next presidential election. It would be a sure way of getting Craig elected.

She asked how long it would take to make the breakthrough.

Jorge laughed and said that he had no clue.

Lacey then asked how much money he wanted.

Jorge nodded, looked into his cup, and quietly said that he would like the same funding as she had allocated for the Door program.

Lacey laughed and said that now she understood why he had come to talk to her in person.

Jorge nodded and said that he wanted to be sitting in front of her so that she would see that he was sober and had not gone crazy.

Lacey said that she had to get to another meeting but that his request would be granted but only if he promised that when her term expired she would get to go out to Doorship One and if another breakthrough occurred she would get to also make the leap out into the Universe.

Jorge beamed a smile and said that he would personally see that she got both wishes. He stood up gave her a saluted, wished her a good day and turned and left the room.

Lacey spent the rest of the day going from one meeting to the next but she could not get it out of her mind that she would soon be traveling across the solar system and maybe out into the universe.

She now knew that being President had a benefit that she had not dreamed about before the Door program. It had now become a step beyond anything she had dreamt about that had entered her mind. She was going to make sure the General got the funding he was seeking and that Tom and Linda got a special gift from her as well.

Jorge walked out to the where his car was waiting. He knew that he had sealed the deal for a continuation of both the Door program and now a new venture. He wondered what it should be called. He decided that he would sponsor a contest among his inner circle of Fold leaders to help him think of a name.

He had his support in Lackland set up a special meeting where he planned to share the fact that he had the funding for the new program and at that meeting he would hold a contest to name that program.

Unbeknownst to Jorge, Lydia had called Tom and Linda and asked them about their idea that would lead to leaping across the universe.

Linda responded that she and Tom were just noodling on the concept and throwing the noodles against the wall to see if any of the them would stick.

Lydia laughed and said that they should make sure to use Uncle Ted's cheese sauce so that some of the noodles would stick. She then added that H^3 might help in thinking the concept through. She commented that Joe had gone off talking about folding the fabric of space and creating a hole at the point where the Fold met but she knew that both of them were not the mathematical and physics brains on the team.

The line went silent and then Tom spoke up and asked if he could talk with Joe about what he was thinking.

Linda meanwhile picked up a piece of paper, brought the two edges together and then pushed her finger in the middle until the paper touched. She then pushed a pin through at that point. She taped the edges together and put the paper down in the middle of her desk.

Tom had watched Linda and then went silent as an idea came to mind.

Joe and Lydia sat looking at each other as an erratic and somewhat disjointed conversation took place. They knew that something was going on at Linda and Tom's end of the call.

Linda spoke up and said that she and Tom needed to work on the concept that had just been shared. She promised to call them back if she and Tom came up with anything meaningful but added that Joe's idea was what they were going to pursue.

Joe shook his head; said he had no idea what he had said that triggered the two. He suggested that the two of them go out with their bows and target practice and then go for a ride out to their favorite swim hole. He figured that would erase his confusion and he liked the idea of finishing at the swim hole.

While aiming at the black spot at the center of the target, another thought came to Joe's mind.

He envisioned a blackhole. He imagined being able to look down its center and seeing stars on the other side. He wondered if a blackhole was really a Hole in space or if it was a tunnel to another part of the universe. He also knew that it didn't matter if it was a way to another universe. All known blackholes were many lifetimes away from earth and all would rip apart any spaceship entering it. What was needed was a stable opening that was close to earth where a ship like Doorship One could cross to some point in the universe.

His arrow hit the bullseye and as he walked over to retrieve it he realized that he was in over his head in the concept and he needed to talked to H^3 and get his opinion.

He kept thinking it was not so much about folding space as it was accelerating a part of it the way the matter transmitter accelerated the signal to the next matter assembler and the material that existed at that location followed the assembly instructions.

What if the signal sent to a specific point in space had enough power to open a portal to a specific location in a faraway part of the universe and what if that signal was being broadcast from the nose of a spacecraft? If the portal opened, the craft would be able to transit through.

He called H^3 and after a quick explanation of what was going on, he shared his idea.

H^3 was quiet for a moment and then he asked if he had any idea the equation and the power that Tom was using to send the Door transmit instructions.

Joe shook his head and then realized that he was just on the phone. He gave a short laugh and replied that he had no idea.

H^3 said that if Tom had not figured out how to use the power released by the object being disassembled he would have turned the lights of San Jose off. So, the power to send a Doorship through a hole created in space had to be much greater. Where to get that power was going to be a challenge but first the algorithm to create the hole needed to be defined.

Joe laughed and said that he was going for a ride and hoped that H^3 would figure out what he was talking about.

After hanging up. H^3 shared the conversation with Yara who chuckled and let him know that she supported him but she had been an art major before joining the Door effort.

H^3 nodded and dialed Tom and Linda's number.

Tom and Linda were celebrating the news they had just received from Jorge that President McAdam had promised to fund their new break through idea when they answered the phone and heard H^3's voice. After getting over the shock of listening to him explain his idea of how to create a Hole to far distant locations in the galaxy they were amazed at the concept that was being shared.

Linda immediately saw that Tom had an idea of how to create the Hole generator. She was eager to get off the phone so the two of them could begin the ephemeral dance of ideas. She knew that this time they would be able to throw the mix of noodles and the sauce it was mixed in at the wall and some of the noodles would stick.

Tom asked R^3 to meet them at the Lakland lab so that they could work together.

He looked at Linda and said that he had the equation but she would need to find the source of power that would be needed to be transmitted to a point in space. They needed to get back to the lab and set up an experiment to prove the concept and then they would need to get everything mounted on Doorship One. It had to return to Earth so it could be modified.

He sent a text to Jorge letting him know that he and Linda were on the way to the base. He then called for plane reservations. Finally, he called the lab supervisor in Lakland and asked him to modify the lab with an opening in the wall that faced north out to the desert.

What he had in mind would send an object from Lakland Air Force base in San Antonio to Piñon Canyon Maneuver Site in Colorado. The send should be almost instantaneous if he provided enough power. He let Linda know that as soon as he figured out the amount of power he needed he would make a request for fuel.

Linda asked what kind of fuel he was going to need.

He laughed and said that he was thinking that it would take about a ton for the experiment but he needed to do some detailed calculations. He added that he was going to enroll H^3 in validating his equations.

He then said that they needed to pack and get to the airport.

2 Only If

3

<u>Hole to Pinyon Canyon</u>

Jorge got Tom's text as he was flying back to Lakland. He knew that he had opened a new program and it was taking off as fast as the Door program had. He had to come up with a new name for the program. As soon as he got back he was going to somehow come up with that name.

He landed in time to get home for dinner. When he got to his house, Jimena asked him how his trip had been. He responded that it was very much like the time when he had first been awarded that role of leading the Door program. He figured it would be just as challenging and maybe more. He described the new goal and said that he was having a hard time giving the new program a name.

Jimena laughed and said he should call it a hole in one.

Jorge stopped as a flash seemed to cross his mind. No not a hole in one but "The Hole." He had The Door that was opening the way across the solar system and now he was going to have "The Hole" that would go to another part of the universe. The Hole, yes The Hole!

The T-bone steak that Jimena put on the table seemed to be one of the best he had ever tasted. It had been sent by Uncle Ted and had been marinated in one of his secret sauces. He knew that Jimena had frequent sessions with him to discuss various recipes that she had garnered from him.

He had also been told by President McAdam that Uncle Ted had been invited to the White House several times to work with the White House chef so that the favorite "Uncle Ted" dishes she had enjoyed would be available to her at her pleasure. Jorge knew that Joe's father and his uncle both enjoyed their close relationship with the US President.

Jorge leaned back and congratulated Jimena on the great dinner and let her know that the name for the new project was going to be "The Hole."

Jimena laughed and warned him not to fall into it.

Jorge had a day's grace before the members of what he was thinking of as the team that would work on, "The Hole" all converged at the site.

Joe and Lydia were driving in from the ranch.

Tom and Linda were flying in from Heathrow.

H^3 and Yara were flying in from their home in Puget Sound.

Darian and Samantha were flying in from New England where they lived in the home Samantha had grown up in.

He spent the day making sure that their accommodations were spotless and that their favorite foods and beverages were in the refrigerators. He felt more like a travel guide than a general. It actually made him feel just as useful.

Joe and Lydia were the first to arrive. The gate guard had instructions to send them to his office. When they entered he greeted them by giving each a hug and thanking them for the care packages that came regularly from their ranch.

Lydia laughed and replied that they had nothing to do with what Uncle Ted was regularly sending to Jimena. She added that he was currently giving Jimena lessons on various dishes and that the two spent many hours cooking together. She then said that she hoped that those days were as special for him as they were for she and Joe because it always resulted in a great meal.

Jorge smiled and said that explained the once-a-week special meal that Jimena had been treating him to.

The next arrivals all seemed to arrive at once. Linda, Tom, H^3, Yara, Samatha and Darian all arrived within thirty minutes of each other. His office became the center of a get together as everyone greeted each other. There was the crescendo of the initial arrival. The excited discussion about the new project and then like a strong tide receding from the shore, everyone said they were looking to get to their residences, taking a long hot shower and then getting a good night's sleep.

Jorge sat for a moment in his empty office and then decided that he would go home, take a hot shower, enjoy whatever Jimena might have for dinner and then sit with a glass of wine and continue reading, "The Fold" a fiction story about folding the fabric of time and space.

Tom and Linda left the office and drove to their new lab that was still in building thirty nine. They both wanted to see how the modifications that they had requested were going. They knew it had been only a couple of days since they had communicated the changes that they wanted to make and figured that getting an early peek would give them a sense of how long it would take to get the changes made.

They were glad that they had chosen to go to the lab first. The wall that they wanted opened up was in the process of getting the bricks removed. They were able to talk to the construction manager and clarify that they wanted an automated opening and closing panel. They also wanted to have the barrel of what they were calling their hole projector to be automated like a sophisticated modern Whitworth rifle that would have exceptional accuracy over great distances. Its firing mechanism still needed to be worked out but the two were sure they would be firing a laser like beam meant to create the opening in the fabric of space.

Linda sighed as they left the lab and commented that once again they were getting the hardware created before they had the math and the physics developed.

Tom nodded in agreement and added that this time he was going to use inanimate objects versus mice while he developed and tested out his theories. He added that he was still having nightmares about the nine hundred ninety nine mice he had vaporized in developing the Door technology.

The next day the team gathered in the large meeting room on the second floor of the lab building. The view out the window was in the direction that the hole generator would be aiming. Tom pointed out the window and commented that success would be to punch a hole to Piñon Canyon, Colorado.

Linda added that she and Tom had stopped by the previous evening to see how the work in the lab was going. She added that the fuel for what she was calling the "hole cannon" was going to be lead. She added that the same transformation process that was used in the Door transmitter would be used to generate the power that would create the hole, then a secondary projection mechanism similar to a long range missel launcher would fire an object through the hole. This launcher was simulating a rocket ship making the transition through the hole. For the simulation it required much less fuel but it would also use lead as the fuel.

Darian commented that in their case they were not turning lead into gold but lead into pure energy. He smiled and said that he would have liked to see them create gold. He finished by saying what they were creating would just go puff.

Tom commented that he was taking the precaution of having a blast wall built in front of the lab control console.

Joe asked where the hole cannon would be located when it was put on Doorship One.

Linda smiled and said that it would be mounted on the center of wheel that Doorship One formed and it would spin with the wheel. The boost power to move Doorship One through the hole would be a series of small cannons mounted at each joint of the Doorship and would fire backward and launch it through the hole.

H^3 spoke up and said that he was working on how much lead fuel would be required to achieve punching the Hole and how much was required to send the object through the Hole. He added that the math that had been used to transport a human via the Door was extremely complex. He wondered out loud how Linda and Tom had been able to come up with such a complex mathematical description of the transformation process. He said that Tom should stop fretting about the mice because he would most likely had killed ten times that many.

Linda commented that the nine hundred and ninety nine mice that had died as she and Tom experimentally determined what the required energy needed to be to transport them. It turned out that the amount of incremental power was only twenty percent more than the conversion of the mouse's body to energy. That ratio was used to increase the power as they transported each bigger animal that followed and that approach had worked.

She added that by the time they got to the point when Lydia was transported they had refined the power need to where they were one hundred percent certain they had the transport as close to ideal that they possibly could make it. So, it was not so much their math genius as it was the sacrifice of the mice.

Lydia laughed and said that Joe had convinced her that since a pig had survived the transport it was up to her to survive it for the human population. She hoped that the Hole punching would follow the same step by step development process that had been followed in the development of the Door transmitter and by the time she and the team went through they would not end up like sacrificial mice.

Tom nodded and said that he was not going to repeat killing nine hundred and ninety nine mice but he would make sure that everything he knew how to do to make it safe both during the development and the subsequent first actual use would get done.

Late that afternoon H^3 said that he had the initially required hole punching fuel load calculated. He commented that three tons of lead would be used to punch the hole but only two hundred pounds of lead fuel would be needed to send the rocket through the hole.

Linda commented that based on H^3's calculations three tons of lead would require a cannon bore that was ten inches in diameter and forty inches in length. She added that she was going to specify that the cannon wall thickness was to be four inches of the strongest steel available. She wondered what kind of a blast would be generated.

3 Hole to Pinyon Canyon

Yara said that the object launcher would only be using two hundred pounds of lead and would result in a significantly smaller cannon that would be eighteen inches long and only have a three inch bore.

Tom shook his head in dismay. He said that the hole punch cannon barrel energy release would equal an instantaneous energy release that would be equal to thirty years of power generated by an electric generating wind turbine. He said that he was changing the design of the lab into a bomb handling facility and there would be a three foot thick explosion wall between he and the Hole punching and the object launching equipment. He was also making the whole building off limits to everyone during any testing.

Joe commented that he would be glad to watch from afar.

Linda suggested that the team be at the Piñon Canyon facility to verify the arrival of the object that would be sent through the hole. She, Tom and H^3 would be behind the blast wall.

Jorge and Jerald decided that going on their rotation out to Doorship One was a good thing to do while the team initiated the work on the "Hole" project. There was enough construction work and preparation that they figured that they could do their thirty day tour as Doorship One made its way back to Earth in preparation to get retrofitted to make the jump through the Hole that they hoped would be created by the invention of the contraption that Linda and Tom were working on.

The lab in building thirty underwent a very significant modification. The three foot thick steel reinforced explosion wall was build the length of the lab. Behind it the entire control system electronics was put in and wired through underground conduits to the side where the Hole generating cannon and the rocket launch tube were located. The rocket launch tube was small enough that it was placed directly beneath the Hole generating cannon. The setup looked like a giant hovering over a midget. It brought a laugh out of the whole team when they saw the setup.

Darian commented that he saw a St. Bernard and a small terrier standing between its legs.

The work went on twenty for seven but still took more than three weeks to complete.

As the time drew near, Joe and Lydia spent their time arranging with the a tracking crew to monitor and track the flight of the projectile that would be launched through the hole. The tracking was not going to be of the conventional type since the projectile in essence would not be flying through the air but should instantly appear at the designated target area.

What they arranged was for a satellite to pass over the path of what the trajectory would be if it was a rocket but it was to be sensing for an appearance of an object at the target location. They arranged with Tom to put a signal transmitter on that object so that if it fell short it could be found.

3 Hole to Pinyon Canyon

Jorge was informed two days before the test and linked in to the view the action. He and Jerry decided that they would make the launch a celebration on board Doorship One that they would enjoy with popcorn and a bottle of Pellegrino.

4

<u>Failure in the Highest Degree</u>

Tom, Linda, and H³ were the only persons in building thirty one as they took their positions along the control equipment consul.

Linda had arranged for the firefighting squad that normally was stationed out by the base airfield to park nearby about a block away. The rest of the team was at the Piñon Canyon facility in a meeting room.

At Piñon Canyon there was a camera trained on the landing site that was being projected on the meeting room screen. It was the same view that Jorge and Jerry saw on their screen on Doorship One.

Eight in the morning mountain time was the time the test was to take place. The day opened in with radiant streaks the morning sun breaking through the puffy clouds. A warm breeze blew through the trees and the ruffled leaves made it seem like the trees were waving to everyone.

Tom, Linda and H³ had shared an early morning breakfast at the Cantine and then walked to the lab together. They had commented on the gorgeous day and hoped that it was a sign of success.

4 Failure in the Highest Degree

Tom took the seat at the main controls, Linda and H^3 sat in front of the monitoring screens. One screen was focused on the equipment on the other side of the blast wall and the second screen was focused on the landing site. Tom had selected to send a miniature model of Doorship One through the Hole.

He had outfitted the model with a Hole blasting cannon and six propulsion cannons. It was an exact replica of what he figured the actual Doorship would look after retrofitting.

Both Linda and H^3 complimented him on getting the model built and ready for the test. The model was small since it had to fit in the barrel of ship launch cannon. They each held the small model in their hands and admired the detail that the model builder had been able to put into it. The model sat on a locator beacon module that was longer, larger, and noticeably heavier than the model itself.

H^3 loaded the model and the beacon module; into the through the Hole cannon and then went behind the blast wall.

Joe and the rest of the team had all flown to the Piñon Canyon facility where they had been greeted by a Colonel Sanderson who identified himself as the commander of the facility.

It did not take him long to creep out Lydia, Yara and Samantha with his fawning behavior. He seemed bent on ingratiating himself with them as if they were at some drinking party and looking for someone to dance with or to leave with.

It was Samantha that labeled him as weird.

Aliens We

Just before the test, Tom announced that the count down for the test was starting. He put on Tchaikovsky's 1812 Overture and then began a very thorough check of all the control systems and went over the equations associated with the creation of the Hole.

As soon as the music began to play Lydia commented that they had about fifteen minutes before Tom would push the launch button.

Samantha asked how Lydia would know that.

Joe smiled and said that the overture ended with cannon fire and he too was sure that Tom would push the Hole creation button as the cannons fired.

Darian chuckled and said that he needed to learn more about classical music.

As the overture came to an end, Tom looked over to where Linda and H^3 were sitting, smiled, and pushed the button as the cannons began to fire. The air around them seemed come alive, pull away as a deafening roar overwhelm him and knocked him over.

Tom looked over to see both Linda and H^3 laying on the floor with the two computer screens on top of them. He looked up and saw that the blast wall was hovering above him and looking like a slinky that was about to fold over on top of him. He rolled up on his knees and crawled over to Linda.

Linda looked up at the sky and began to laugh hysterically. She was looking up at the clouds and the morning sun breaking through them. She shouted out that the building had vanished. She rolled over and saw that they were all laying on the cement slab that was the floor of the lab and there was no building anywhere to be seen.

4 Failure in the Highest Degree

The fire rescue team watched from their vehicles as the building shell lifted off of its foundation as if it was a butterfly flying away. The blast wave seemed to clear the way through the trees as the building flew through the air towards the edge of the base and landed just inside of the fence line. There was no fire. There was no building to catch fire. There were no trees left standing in a circle that reached the front bumper of the fire truck. The driver excitedly shouted that had they parked any closer they would have followed the building.

All the members in the rescue team ran toward the location where the building had stood. They were expecting to find the bodies of the three scientists that were running some secret test. They were amazed to see three individuals hugging each other and laughing hysterically as they slowly walked around the blast wall.

The ambulance drove up to the three and asked them to sit down so they could get checked out. It was immediately clear that all three were having trouble hearing. A quick examination of their ears cleared them of having any ruptured ear drums. One of the medics commented that it was a miracle. Another nodded and added that finding all three alive made it a miracle.

Tom got up and said that he needed to get a quick look at what was left of the equipment. The main hole creation cannon was still in one piece but the fuel holding chamber did not exist. The propulsion cannon and its fuel chamber seemed to be undamaged. He went to where his control equipment was located and felt relieved that other than the wiring leading to it, the equipment seemed undamaged.

The wire conduit had acted like a cannon that fired all the wiring out beneath the raised floor and out across the lawn where it had landed and looked like a huge pile of snakes twisted together.

Linda and H^3 had joined him and they commented that the blast wall had done its job, but it was about to fall over on its own.

When the overture ended and the cannons went off, Lydia immediately commented that something had gone wrong. She immediately dialed H^3's number. It rang but there was no answer. She dialed Linda's number and again got no answer.

She tried H^3 again and a strange voice answered. Her heart sank until the person said that everything was OK but the person she was ringing could not hear the ring because the explosion had been so loud that he was temporarily deaf. He then explained what had happened to building thirty.

Joe got a call from Doorship One asking what had happened. He put Lydia on the call and listened as she explained that a huge explosion had eliminated building thirty but Tom, Linda and H^3 were all safe.

Yara had tears in her eyes as she listened to the exchange. She had wanted to stay with H^3 but had been told that she should be with the rest of the team at the site where the object coming through the Hole would end up.

Later after the call, the object was found because its locating signal transmitter had survived but it had traveled at least three times farther than planned and was sending a signal from deep in Canada's Northwest Territory. It was only located because the observation satellite passing over it received the locater signal and logged its coordinates.

When Jorge realized what had happened he let Jerry know that he was going to be left at the helm and would be bringing Doorship One into orbit around Earth on his own. Jorge then transported back to Lakland and immediately went to the site where the rescue team was still attending to Linda, H^3 and Tom.

He was in civilian clothes, was not immediately recognized and stopped by one of the rescue squad. He identified himself and apologized for being out of uniform but he had responded immediately upon learning of the situation. He went over to Tom and asked him what had happened.

Tom pointed to his ear and gave him a pad and pencil.

He wrote, "What happened?"

Tom shook his head and wrote back, "Too much fuel," and drew a smiley face after it.

Jorge could not help but laugh as he took in the totality of the missing building, the downed trees and bent over light poles. Too much fuel was the answer! So much fuel that there was a three football field diameter circle that had been flattened and burned.

He was just walking with the three to his car when a call came in from Joe to let him know that the Doorship One model that had been sent through the Hole had been located in the Canadian Northwest Territory. He laughed and said that the Hole opening had been much farther north than anticipated. He and Lydia were going to fly there with an RCMP escort and retrieve it. He added that the rest of team was returning to the base.

It was three days later when Tom and Linda met with Jorge in his office. They both apologized for having demolished an entire building on their first trial, but they had successfully created a Hole and had put their spaceship model through it.

Jorge congratulated them and said that he was going to let the two of them give the President an update to the progress and he hoped that she would think it as funny as he did.

Linda nodded and said that she and Tom had agreed to set up the next experiment at the same location but with no building. She had designed a three-foot thick, steel reinforced, horseshoe enclosure for the hole punching cannon and another three foot thick steel reinforced explosion wall behind it where she, Tom and H^3 had agreed they would sit. She added that H^3 was determining how much to reduce the amount of fuel based on the location where their model of Doorship One had landed.

The phone rang and Jorge after a quick hello put the President on the speaker phone.

4 Failure in the Highest Degree

Lacey was sitting with Vice President Lebak in the Oval Office. She began by saying she was glad to hear that the three of them had survived an explosion that had eliminated an entire thirty thousand square foot building. She then asked what had happened.

H^3 identified himself and said that it was his fault and he was going over the fuel requirement calculation trying to determine how he could have made such a grievous error.

Linda spoke up and said that it was not H^3's fault and that she had been the one that had specified how many tons of lead would be needed to provide the required hole punching power.

Vice President Lebak identified himself, gave a chuckle and said that there certainly had been sufficient punch to the generate the Hole. He added that he had negotiated with the Canadian prime minister to get the object back. He said that the prime minister had laughed, then asked why the US was launching miniature replicas of Doorship One and polluting the pristine Canadian wilderness.

Tom spoke up and said that the model was his idea but he would let the blame for having polluted the Canadian wilderness rest on Linda's and H^3 shoulders. He added he was also blaming them for his potential hearing loss as well as the disappearance of an entire building that he had become fond of.

That caused the President to comment that she now understood her favorite General's problem of dealing with the geniuses on his team. She reiterated her pleasure in hearing that everyone was alright and asked where her favorite team members, Joe and Lydia were when all of this had happened.

Jorge commented that they had been at the site where the object was supposed to have landed, then they had gone to the Canadian Wilderness to retrieve the Doorship One model and they were now on their way back as they spoke.

The President ended by saying it sounded like a new technology had literally exploded onto the scene and that she was going to be the proud supporter of that breakthrough. She suggested that Tom and Linda build a very thick blast shield that would survive all additional tests and that H^3 get the fuel quantity trimmed sufficiently back.

Jorge smiled as he hung up the phone. He said that he was hosting a grill out at his place as soon as the new launch facility was built and added that he was inviting Uncle Ted and Joe's father. He added that he was confident that his wife and Uncle Ted would be collaborating on the entire meal plan. He commented that by that time the entire team would at the grill out and Doorship One would be back in Earth orbit so Jerry could join in.

Tom smiled and commented that this time he had not killed one living thing.

Linda corrected him and said that all the oak and maple trees had been reduced to less than saw dust and the lawn around building thirty had been burned to a crisp and if their had been any small animal life in the trees or on the ground they had all perished. She was sure they had matched and exceeded killing nine hundred and ninety nine dead mice.

4 Failure in the Highest Degree

H^3 commented that he was going to figure out how far the three tons of lead had sent the hole and scale it back so they would exactly hit the target the next time. He hoped that the tremendous blast that had been generated could be better controlled. He added that even with the fuel reduction, they needed a better way to contain the tremendous blast that it would produce.

Linda nodded and said that she would work on some sort of way to contain the blast. She added that in space it would look spectacular but pose little problem since it had an infinite volume to spread into.

She said that she planned to make the blast follow a wide horseshoe blast shield guide that would blow out to the front of the hole-generation cannon area into a multi paneled diffuser on each side. The horseshoe guide would be three feet of reinforced concrete with a blast top that would also guide the blast into a top diffuser.

Tom said that the diffuser design sounded great and he planned to put a three foot thick shield immediately behind the horseshoe guide to protect them and all the equipment. It would have a similar reinforced roof and be closed in back by a thick plexiglass wall.

He added that they would not replace any of the building and they would make sure that the conduit coming back from the Hole cannon and the ship launcher would guide any blast traveling through them out beneath and behind the control center.

Jorge was pleased with the approach that allowed them to quickly proceed. It was clear to him that the approach being suggested could be accomplished within two weeks. This meant a minimum of development delay and it hardly impacted the short term budget. Long term it would cost him close to fifty million to replace the building that no longer existed. He was likely never to replace it since it had been around for more than fifty years and had hardly been used until the Fold project and now the Hole Project had come along.

Joe and Lydia returned and after delivering the small model of Doorship One they went back to the ranch in Canadian, Texas.

4 Failure in the Highest Degree

5

<u>Success with a……</u>

The following weeks saw Tom, Linda and H^3 working from home as they reviewed the Hole generation equations that guided the Hole generation cannon's energy release. They were all trying to make sense of the efficiency of the lead molecules conversion into energy. There were several ways that the energy generation could fluctuate up or down. It depended greatly on the exact starting temperature of the lead. It seemed very sensitive to just a few degrees in either direction. They came to agreement to have the lead at as close to minus four hundred fifty five degrees Fahrenheit as they could achieve within a reasonable time and power draw. After checking out the tremendous amount of power needed to take three tons of lead down to that temperature they decided that they would settle for a minus fifty degrees. This left them somewhat in the dark exactly how much energy would be generated as they converted the lead to energy.

Linda commented that she was going to make sure that extra reinforcement was put into the blast walls.

Jorge and Jerry made daily trips out to where the preparation for the next test was taking place. They marveled at the transformation that the location was undergoing. At one time the area had resembled a park where families might come for a picnic.

Jerry commented that the transformation seemed to resemble what the Maginot (pronounced Madge-in-O) fortification line in France looked like. The only thing missing were the huge cannons aimed into Germany.

Jorge was glad that the horseshoe was aligned with the empty desert north of the base. He at least was not risking any of the homes near the base. He also liked the high horse shaped dirt blast wall that had been put in place around the entire Hole cannon area. Its design was similar to the barriers put up at bomb making facilities to guide a blast upward.

Jerry commented that he was impressed at the speed with which Tom and Linda were getting the test facility built.

Jorge led the way into the shield maze in front of the blast wall. It was meant to diffuse the blast that would be guided into them. He commented that blast shields seemed to be built to collapse as each panel absorbed the blast.

Jerry said that he hoped there were enough panels to contain the blast.

Linda had watched the two go into the blast field in front of the Hole generation cannon. As they came out she asked them what they thought and laughed when Jorge made the comparison of the place to the Maginot fortification.

She said that's what she hoped the shields would contain any blast that resulted and no one on base would be hurt. She added that she felt lucky to have survived the first blast and was still getting over the ringing in her ears. She was doing everything possible not to have a similar experience again.

H^3 was sitting at the new control panel getting acclimated to the set up. He was still not sure that the fuel loading was quite right but he felt that it was close. He hoped that the second trial would not be quite as wild as the first one had been.

The entire team met each morning to discuss the progress that was being made.

Ryan had resumed his planner's role and was tracking the progress being made with the rebuilding of the site. He spent almost every hour of the day tracking the construction progress that was being made and preparing his progress report for the next morning. It was clear to him that the contractor was doing everything possible to get the construction done post haste.

The concrete cure time was the time bottleneck. He laughed when he made the report that the only thing slower than cement curing was the lead that was being cooled. It seemed that it was limited by the amount of energy that could be provided to the cooling units.

Each morning Tom would report that he had planted another tree to make up for the ones that had been destroyed. He commented that there was nothing else for him to do before the next test.

H^3 reported that he continued to work his way through the transformation of lead to energy equations and the conversion efficiency would depend on the final temperature that the lead reached before the next test.

Each morning Linda brought in a batch of cookies, muffins, and pies that she had baked the night before. She admitted that she was getting nervous about the upcoming test and that she was really disturbed with Ryan's poor management of the time for the cement to cure, the time it was taking to cool the lead and that he was risking his job by not pushing both along at a faster pace.

Jorge enjoyed the joking that his two mad scientist were demonstrating and knew that the next test would be the moment that they received the word that the concrete had reached the design structural strength that was expected. He looked at Ryan and asked him as to the date that the curing curve pointed to.

Ryan responded that it appeared that in three days the concrete would reach its design structural strength.

Jorge announced that the next test would be in five days. He said that the two day grace period would give everyone involved a chance to be in place. He suggested that for this test only Joe and Lydia go to the target site. The rest of the team should join him in the meeting room, that he had been assured was beyond the blast circumference and monitor the test from there. Refreshments would be on hand and depending on the timing and the test outcome lunch would also be provided.

Joe and Lydia had been enjoying their time on the ranch. It was a great place for them to relax and prepare for the next adventure that both were sure was about to happen.

Joe was enjoying his time developing his cooking skills by working with Uncle Ted. He liked the way the two of them got along in the kitchen and how Uncle Ted was coaching him on developing his cooking skills. Uncle Ted kept saying that cooking was a man's best way into a woman's heart.

Lydia spent a great deal of time with Joe's father. The two of them would take walks that seemed to take on a theme that they pursued on each walk. It was clear to her that Trey would always test the water with a topic he had in mind and if she responded positively he would continue to develop that discussion. It was also clear to her that her father in law had a very broad range of knowledge that he had nurtured and developed. She thought of him as an older version of Joe and his very deep mind.

Her brother had come out for the summer to work on the ranch. It was clear to her that he was maturing and reaching a level of self-confidence that she had not seen before. When it got close to the time for him to return to school, the two of them took a trip home to Tennessee where she spent a week with her mother and father.

Joe had accompanied them.

She was pleased with how well he interacted with both her mother and father. It surprised her when he volunteered to prepare a special meal. He and her mother went out to buy the fixings and then the two worked for much of the afternoon preparing. She watched as the filet was seasoned with salt and put in the refrigerate for an hour. Then Joe took it out and patted the filets dry and threw the five into the large skillet, seared them for three minutes per side. Then Joe spooned in butter to the point that the steaks were surrounded and simmering. When the butter began to smoke he turned off the burner, flipped the steaks and then put them on the serving platter and put one parsley branch on each steak as garnish.

He then took the baked potatoes out of the oven split them open, put butter into each of them and then put them on a serving platter.

Her mother had set the table and prepared a mixed vegetable salad that she put into individual serving bowls.

The two put everything on the table and called everyone to dinner.

Her father lead a short prayer and then asked what wine each person wanted.

The dinner turned out to be one of the best that she had ever eaten.

The next day her brother left for school and the following morning she and Joe headed to Piñon Canyon. They would be there to retrieve the model of the Doorship that would be shot through the hole. They joked about the fact that the last time Tom had missed the target by about half a continent.

They both wondered if H^3's recalculation of the amount of lead fuel would be accurate enough that the hole would be punched through and would deliver the model of Doorship One to the Piñon Canyon location. They were counting on Tom, Linda and H^3 getting the Hole creation controlled. They knew that they and their team would be the ones that would take Doorship One through the Hole once the concept was proven. They wanted to be able to go and then be able to return from the through Hole in space.

Tom and Linda were having the same discussion about getting the math equations right. Tom shook his head as he admitted that somehow they had been a magnitude of order off on their first calculation.

Linda said that it was her fault for miscalculating the energy release of converting the lead to energy. It turned out that the initial temperature of the lead was much more critical than she had anticipated. She had worked with H^3 to get a better handle on that aspect but both of them felt unsure about how accurately they had done that. Additionally getting the lead as cold as possible while it was on earth would take so much energy that all the electrical power the state of Texas was capable of generating would not be enough to get the lead to minus four hundred fifty seven degrees. They both agreed that once in space the lead could reach close to that temperature in less than a week just by being kept out in space.

5 Success with a……

Jorge was well aware that his three genius scientists were counting on success. They had requested that the lead be launched and stored strategically at the center of Doorship One. They had also given him drawings of the modification to the center of Doorship One's wheel location where the Hole generation cannon would be located and the fuel chamber where the super cold lead would be stored. There were the six small lead powered rockets that were to be mounted at each wheel joint location that would propel Doorship One through the hole.

He had authorized the launching of the lead and the modification work to begin. He hoped that the coming test was successful. The modification work was estimated to take at least a month.

On the morning of the test, Linda, Tom and H^3 had breakfast together at the base's cafeteria.

As usual they were escorted by three guards that had become their escorts since the time when Joe, Lydia, and Darian had been kidnapped. They had made arrangements that the guards would be located well away from the test location.

They were dropped off at the test location and entered the explosion proof control room and made sure everything was as expected.

Tom greeted everyone that was watching the test. He had been informed that the President and her cabinet members had decided to watch the trial. She briefly said good morning and wished them good luck.

Jorge was in his office with Darian, Samantha and Yara.

Lydia and Joe said they were at the Piñon Canyon facility and had cameras trained on the target location.

Tom looked at Linda and H^3 and asked if they were ready.

Linda put on her hearing protection and said that she was.

H^3 did the same and said, "ditto."

Tom pressed a huge button that he had made for the occasion and

……

5 Success with a……

6

.......A Huge Blast

There was a moments delay and then the resulting blast leveled the shields located in front of the test area. The control room they were in shook and the three had to stand and hold on to the consul in front of them. This time the structures held but the control system connection to the Hole generation unit was fried. The cameras trained on the Hole generation equipment went blank as the blast took them out.

The silence that followed seemed to last forever. Then they heard Lydia shout that Tom had missed by the length of three football fields but they had the location where the model had landed. Joe added that unfortunately it was buried underground but the beacon was working and they would retrieve it.

Tom let out a cheer, grabbed Linda and H^3 and danced around with them in celebration. It was clear to everyone that success had been achieved.

The President, who was viewing the test from the White House, laughed and said that she had never seen such destruction called a success. She added that she guessed that congratulations were in order and it was time for her to get back to more controlled though still very chaotic work.

When she hung up she looked around the room and asked what everyone thought about the new capability that the US had just obtained. There was silence. Her scientific advisor finally spoke up and asked if the speed of the object had been tracked to see how fast it was moving.

She smiled and said that there was no way to track the object since it really did not travel but went through a hole in the fabric of space. She added that when they dug up the object that had gone through that hole, even though it might be in the middle of a granite boulder, it would be whole and in the same condition as when it went through the Hole. She added that the three scientists that were dancing to celebrate their success were doing so because they had achieved a historic breakthrough.

She then looked at her scientific advisor and suggested that he visit the Lakland facility and learn more about the capabilities of the breakthrough. She looked at the Secretary of Defense and suggested he go as well because such capability would greatly affect any missile technology.

Jorge knew that a huge step had been made and said that there would be a celebration at his house the following evening. It had not escaped him that the breakthrough would not only support moving across the Universe and leapfrog the limitation of the speed of light but it would also alter the standing of missile defense and the need to launch missiles at all. He figured that the President was too smart to miss that aspect of the breakthrough. He had just finished the thought when his support let him know that the Secretary of Defense was asking for a good time to meet with him.

At the next meeting in his office, H^3 said that they needed to do one more test to see if they could get a better handle on the energy release of the transformation of lead to energy. He said that they had fallen short of their target by a very small fraction but that fraction would be magnified greatly as they traversed the millions to billions of miles across the Universe.

Joe and Lydia were both sitting on the back tail gate of the grey pickup watching the backhoe dig down into the ground. An Army team was deployed around the site as if there was going to be an attack. Joe commented that he was pleased with the serious nature that the site commander had adopted since the last time they had been there. He was sure that the top brass had been appraised of the important nature of the test that was going on and the Colonel had decided to act accordingly.

Lydia agreed and said that she figured that having the President be part of the observation team had made the point that the project was of national importance. If nothing else her interest had made it important through the Army ranks. The Marine and Airforce ranks had already understood the situation from their experience with the development of the Door technology. This was the first time the Army had been involve.

She did not say anything about Colonel Sanderson's sexist behavior and his trying ingratiate himself to her. It creeped her out.

The backhoe operator rested the bucket on the pile he had built and shouted that it was time to dig with shovels. A second backhoe put a steel shell down into the hole and three men with shovels were lowered in.

Joe and Lydia walked over to the edge and looked down the ten feet to where the three were now digging.

Lydia commented that ten feet was deeper than she had imagined.

The digging went on for a good twenty minutes before one of the diggers stop and pointed to a boulder. The digging now took on a different nature. Two additional men were lowered into the hole and they each began digging with a red handled hand trowel and a small spade. They carefully exposed the Doorship One Model that was embedded half way in the black and light green streaked amphibolite boulder. They dug around the boulder until it was entirely exposed.

Joe was asked how he wanted to handle the situation.

Joe looked at Lydia and said that they should take the boulder with the embedded model back to Lakland.

Lydia nodded. She commented that the sight of the model embedded in the boulder gave her pause when she thought about the jump across the distances that were being contemplated and that they needed to figure out a way to send out scouts that could make certain they would not end up in the middle of some planet or star.

Back at Lakland, Jorge was walking the blast area with Jerry. The two realized that the blast diffusers had done their job but they were not strong enough to withstand the power of the blast.

Tom and Linda came out from where the hole cannon was located and commented that their second attempt had been dramatically better than the first one but they still did not have a handle on the power that they were manipulating.

H^3 joined them and shook his head. He commented that he felt like the time he had failed to solve a math problem because he had inadvertently put in a minus versus a plus sign. He commented that the next test needed to be dead on because if they could not get the math right at the miniscule distance they were dealing with versus the billions of miles in the universe they were condemning the people making such a trip to a certain death. He smiled and said that since he was one of them he was going to make certain he got the math right.

Jorge nodded. He shared a photo showing the model embedded in the boulder. He commented that not only did the program need to become more accurate but it had to make sure not to launch the Doorship across the universe into some planet or star.

6......A Huge Blast

Tom looked at Linda and commented that they needed to think about how to scout out the area where the Doorship would be going.

Linda replied that they needed to send out a scout to verify the location before they sent the actual ship through the hole.

Tom asked how long the hole would stay open.

H^3 said that he had no clue about how long the opening would stay. He added that they would need to send a scout through first to ensure a clear hole landing area then they could worry about how long a hole would remain in existence.

He added that he was also worried about how to be more accurate. He figured it would have to do with the speed of the lead fuel to energy conversion.

Jorge laughed and said that from what he had observed the Doorship model transfer through the hole seemed to be almost instantaneous.

H^3 nodded and said that he agreed but he was thinking in terms of nano seconds; make the hole, send a scout through, receive a go signal from the scout, send the Doorship through. The total time would be around ten microseconds. This was the kind of precision that was needed to make the program a success.

Linda shook her head and said that some significant equipment improvement was going to be necessary. She wondered if Aaron could join the team and improve the programing so they could achieve the accuracy and the speed that they needed.

Jorge nodded and said that he would arrange for Aaron to join the Hole team. He added that he hoped that the next several tests would resolve the accuracy problem and he hoped that the problem with blowing up the equipment could also be resolved before they put it on Doorship One.

As he and Jerry walked back to his car, Jerry commented that he had several power system experts that might be able to resolve the problem of burning up the equipment.

Jorge immediately said he would love for them to join in. The three geniuses needed some practical design help. He added that he was also going to make sure that Ryan McComber would continue to manage the effort like a formal project. He was not going to allow another test until the team came together and coalesced around a solid execution plan. He was going to insist on an organized approach to the next few tests.

That afternoon Lydia and Joe arrived. They had the boulder taken directly to Jorge's office. It had been cleaned and looked like the main model in a feature movie.

Jorge stood looking at it and said that he was going to have it mounted on a pedestal and put in the main entrance to the building. He then looked at Lydia and asked if she was still game on being first to try this with Doorship One.

Lydia smiled as she replied that there needed to be some refinement in the process before they tried it with a real ship and real people.

Joe added that shooting from the hip had gotten them close but a great deal of refinement needed to happen.

Jorge agreed and said that in the morning the entire team with some of the original Door team members would be joining the Hole effort.

The next morning as each person entered the room and their eyes rested on the boulder with the model half embedded in the boulder they stopped and as if hypnotized they walked over to it and stood looking. It was a grim reminder of what could happen.

When Tom and Linda walked into the room they recognized the members that had been on the Door program team and knew that Jorge wanted the Hole program to get organized. They looked at each other, smiled and quietly mouthed, "Thank God." They knew that they had been lucky to have winged it through two tests. They liked that Jorge was reconstituting the effort by adding the people that had made the Door program successful.

H^3 smiled and commented that he now knew an individual who knew how to make decisions in Nano seconds. He added that working for the Nano Second King was a great relief.

Jorge called the meeting to order and announced that there would be no more Hole generation tests until the team got organized, the equipment got explosion proofed and the Hole generation equations and programing went through the required refinement. He commented that he had the best in each field in the room.

He looked at Tom and Linda and asked for their reaction.

Linda stood up and walked over to the boulder and put her hand on the model of Doorship One and said that in the development of the Door technology she and Tom had killed nine hundred and ninety nine mice but the Hole technology would not give them that latitude. They could continue testing with a model but when it came time to actually prove it at full scale there would be people she loved at risk and she wanted that risk to be zero.

So, she felt great to have a team that could make that happen being brought together. She looked at Tom and then at the group and said that Tom still had nightmares about having been responsible for killing the mice so I know that he too welcomes everyone on the team with the goal of reducing the risk to zero.

Tom stood up and said that the first two tests were gratifying in the sense that it proved the concept of being able to create a Hole through the fabric of space and time but they also terrified him because it was worse than sending so many mice to their deaths. When the time to send the Doorship through, I want to know that I am sending them through safely. In fact, I intend to be on the Doorship and I want to go and come back. I want to celebrate with all of you.

Jorge smiled and said that they would then look to Ryan and asked him to work with the team and create a master plan and identify the critical path to sending the Doorship safely through to some place in the Universe.

6......A Huge Blast

7

<u>Doorship to Cosmos Odessey</u>

Jorge had been summoned by President McAdams. She indicated she wanted to meet with him and though it was important. He had no idea what she might want that she needed a face to face meeting with him. He had arrived early and had been sitting in a small meeting room somewhere in the White House. He was not sure exactly where he had been taken because the young lady that had guided him to the room had kept talking about the history of the White House and had kept asking him whether he knew about some tidbit or other about its history. Her running dialogue had totally distracted him from his train of thought and he had lost his orientation. The only thing he knew was where the rest room was because it was the last tidbit that she had told him about. The rest room had been installed in eighteen fifty three. His curiosity of whether it still had the original plumbing was satisfied about an hour after he had been left waiting.

It was now almost noon.

He had been in the room wondering whether he had been forgotten when a young Marine Sergeant entered, saluted him, and let him know that he was to escort him to the President's Dining Room located in the northwest corner of the second floor.

He was surprised to learn that he had been sitting only about twenty feet away. He looked out of the window and got his orientation when he realized he was looking out at the North Lawn.

He was shown to his seat by what he thought of as a "black tie" waiter who was wearing a very formal uniform, that consisted of a crisp white shirt, black slacks, a black tie, a vest, and polished black shoes. The name tag over his left pocket let Jorge know that Raymond LeClare was going to serve he and the President lunch.

Raymond pulled out a chair and Jorge took the seat.

He looked around at the rooms décor. The wallpaper depicted various events in the American Revolutionary War. He was not familiar with all the scenes shown on the wall but it was clear to him that it was an extensive display of what had happened during the Revolution. He noted that the window draperies of blue and green silk damask topped by window treatments of green silk with gold bullion fringe seemed to augment the colors of the landscapes. He had just taken in the Turkish rug in a similar color style, that was on the floor when President McAdam was escorted into the room by two men in black suits that he took as body guards.

He stood up and was immediately waved down. As he sat down he listened to the President apologize for making him wait and that she hoped that the delicious lunch would make up for the delay. She smiled and added that the world famous Chef Ted Stratford had prepared Magret de Canard and would be personally serving it.

Jorge gave a small laugh and said that he was sure that lunch would more than make up for the wait. He wondered what Uncle Ted was doing in Washington. He knew he was in a for a great meal. He then asked if he had been invited to lunch or was there something more that Madam President might want.

She smiled and said that the first thing she wanted was for him to call her by her name.

He smiled nodded and said that Lacey it was and what else would she like to ask or tell him.

Lacey smiled and said that they should first enjoy lunch and then she would like an update on the progress of the Hole project. Lacey waved her hand around the room and asked what he thought of the remodeling that she had commissioned. She commented that the wallpaper had been buried beneath several layers of wall covering and had just been restored in the last few months. The two of them were the first to have a meal in the room since the restoration.

Jorge took a minute to look around and then said that the restoration was exceptionally well done because it looked like it was brand new.

Lacey smiled and said that she had hired a young lady that seemed to know a thousand details about the White House that no one else knew who had told her about the wall paper that had been covered over multiple times.

Jorge chuckled and said that he was sure that the young lady that had escorted him to the waiting room was the one Lacey was talking about.

Lacey smiled and asked if he had learned anything about the White House from her.

Jorge smiled and said that indeed he had but he only remembered that the rest room that he had access to was the first one installed in the White House in Eighteen fifty three.

Lacey chuckled and said that every time she interacted with Tracy Minton, the young lady that had escorted him, she learned some new tidbit about the White House.

The conversation ended as lunch arrived. The arrival was led by Uncle Ted wearing the Chef's outfit that Lydia and Joe had given him. He had a broad smile, did a small bow as he announced that he hoped that his Magret de Carnard surrounded by sautéed figs and eggplant would be to their liking. He went on to point at the bottle of Bordeaux and added that it would pair wonderfully with Magret de Canard due to its ripe black fruit and oak tones. He held up the bottle and said that the richness of the duck breast would be complemented its fruity nature.

Jorge took a bite and a rich beefy, slightly gamey flavor of the meat melting in his mouth made him close his eyes and sigh. He shook his head and commented that he thought he had been given a taste of heaven. He watched as a broad smile transformed Uncle Ted and seemed to make him a few inches taller.

Uncle Ted let him know that he would be taking a serving home to Jimena so that she would be able to enjoy it too.

Lacey complemented him on preparing such a wonderful lunch to commemorate the transformation of President's Dining Room.

Once the lunch dishes was removed, Lacey commented that she had invited him to be the first to eat with her in the project that she had undertaken after the last election. She looked at Jorge and said that she wanted to change the name of Doorship One.

Jorge nodded and asked what name she had in mind.

Lacey said that she wanted to formally change the name of Doorship One to Starship One.

Jorge shook his head and asked if that was the reason she had asked him to come to Washington.

Lacey nodded, was silent for a moment and said that she wanted a ride on Starship One when her term as President ended.

Jorge smiled and said that she did not need to wait that long if she could take a few days off and vacation with a team of people who would gladly host her and share lunch. He added that a couple of those people were taking lessons from Chef Ted Stratford and were getting almost as good as he. He went on to add that he liked her idea to rename Doorship One and he would arrange for a renaming ceremony.

Lacey smiled and said that she would likely take him up on his invitation to get a ride before her term ended. She looked at her watch and said that she needed to run and asked that before he left to leave her an update on the current status of the Hole project.

Jorge was escorted by Tracy who continued to educate him about the White House. He asked if she could take him to the kitchen where the food was prepared.

Tracy stopped for a minute, made a call to check on his request and then redirected her dialogue to the history of kitchens in the White House. Jorge patiently listened but what he was really interested in was to congratulate Uncle Ted on the great lunch and to invite him to come to Lakland and be in charge of a dinner to be attended by the President.

He walked out of the White House wishing he could call and let everyone know about his discussion with the President.

Joe and Lidya were aware of where Uncle Ted was. They were not surprised but pleased that the President was recognizing him by her invitation to prepare a special lunch. What neither of them knew was that the lunch would be attended only by Jorge.

The two had decided to spend four days a week at the ranch and three days a week at Lakland. Their focus was on how Doorship One would be controlled as it transitioned through the Hole. There was little to guide them on how the control system would be managed. They went on board Doorship One several times to determine how the ships control system should be modified.

Aaron stood next to Lydia and Joe as they discussed how the Hole cannon and the six through the Hole booster rockets would be controlled and how the controls should be laid out. He always enjoyed working with the two and recognized that Joe had an intuitive feel of how the spinning six sided shape of the Doorship would respond.

Aliens We

He listened as Joe explained how they would be sitting and speculated as to whether there would be a tremendous acceleration thrust. He suggested that they put thrust sensors into the next model to be sent through the Hole so they could determine how the control system should be designed. He was pleased that both Joe and Lydia thanked him. He listened as Joe called Linda and asked her to put the sensors into the model that would be used during the next test.

Ryan worked with everyone to develop the critical plan path to the next test. He was pleased with everyone's thorough participation. When it was all compiled he shared the timing of the critical path which surprised him on how fast the team was working. He laughed a little when Tom complained that the critical path was too long. He then pointed out that he, Tom was the person who was making it the longest.

When he got Joe's call he adjusted the critical path slightly and let Tom know he was no longer the bottleneck but that the instrumentation that needed to be put into the model of Doorship One was.

Jorge called a meeting of the team for the day after his return from his trip to the White House. He had a model of Doorship One covered with a cloth as part of the display that he had set up in the meeting room. There were three models. The first one was the Doorship One model that had been retrieved from Canada. The second one was the model half buried in the granite boulder. The third covered one was a model of the renamed Doorship One to Starship One.

He figured that the meeting would quickly agree to the name change. He called the meeting to order and shared the discussion he had with the President. He then unveiled the renamed model and asked if everyone was in agreement.

Everyone seemed to be nodding in agreement. Lydia looked around and then asked is they were shooting for a star or were they shooting for a galaxy or were they shooting for the universe? What were they shooting for?

Tom looked at her and said that he liked her questions and that it made him think that what he was hoping to do was to open the path to the universe.

Joe nodded and asked if Pathfinder One, Universe One or Cosmos One should all be considered.

Linda smiled and said since they were talking about the name why not call it the McAdam.

Jorge gave a groan and said that he had been hoping for a quick agreement to the name. He asked if they agreed to a name change.

Everyone agreed that a name change was appropriate.

Aaron spoke up and asked if what they were really all on was a wonderful mind expanding Odyssey.

Ryan nodded and suggested that they combine where they were going, the Cosmos with Odyssey and name the ship the "Cosmos Odyssey" and drop the designation of One since they had no idea if there would be other similar vessels.

The room went silent for a moment. Then Linda suggested they put all the names on the white board and each of them would have five votes which they could distribute in any fashion they desired across the six currently proposed names. She didn't wait for an answer but wrote the names down on white board and put her vote on the board.

After everyone voted with their check marks it was clearly obvious that Ryan's suggested name of Cosmos Odyssey was clearly the most popular.

Jorge had put four of his five votes on that name. He asked who was going to tell the President that her name change suggestion had come in a distant fourth.

Joe smiled and said that Jorge was the one that had the wonderful lunch with the President that Uncle Ted had prepared. He reminded him that there were no free lunches and that the cost of that lunch was that it was his responsibility to get that message to the President.

Jorge smiled, nodded, and said that he agreed but he thought that the person who should take the message to the President was her favorite person on the team, Joe Pender Elsinger.

8

<u>**Test Number Three**</u>

Tom, Linda and H^3 were checking the physical changes they had made. The cables to the energy conversion chamber had been resized to be twenty times larger than before. H^3 had insisted on that change. This made those cables eighteen inches in diameter. The cables looked more like pipes than cables. Linda and Tom had modified the speed of lead to energy conversion to be at least one hundred times slower. They hoped that this would lessen the overall explosive nature of the conversion. They had agreed to Jorge's request to triple the size of the blast area diffusion panels because they did not want to spend time to convince him that the increase in the number of diffusion panels were not needed. The power of the Hole opening cannon had been reduced. The three of them were fairly certain that they would open the Hole to exactly the point in Piñon Canyon that they were targeting. The propulsion for the model was modified as well so it would place the model at the surface rather than in the ground. They knew that the model made the jump through the Hole versus a rapid transit across that distance because of the way the second model had become merged with the granite boulder.

The fact that that model had been embedded in the granite stone actually proved the fact that it had traveled through a hole that included the boulder. It also necessitated the need to create scout probes to ensure the location where the model would end up was clear of all obstructions.

Lydia had welcomed their recognition for the need for the all clear scout probes and had suggested six that would verify a clear area at least three times the dimension of the Cosmos Odyssey.

For the coming test there would be two scouts that would go through the hole first and then the model would be sent. If the two scouts did not verify the clearance of the landing site the test would be stopped. Testing the scouts was as important to the test as getting the model through to Lydia. Linda had insisted that the scouts fan out to clear three times the required area that the model would need. There would be six scouts for the actual transition of Cosmos Odyssey through the Hole and they would fan out to verify a clear area three times larger than the area required.

The three of them had agreed that if the next test went as planned they wanted to do three more tests with a day in between to refill the lead conversion chamber. They would focus on automating that feature so that the much larger fuel chamber on Cosmos Odyssey would not need human intervention.

Jerry had been working with scientists in his organization to see how they could improve on the conventional rocket engines that would be used once the Cosmos Odyssey was traveling in normal space. They were working on the fuel efficiency as well as improving the maneuverability of the space wheel. His discussions with the Cosmos Odyssey team led to the idea of small distance Hole blasts that would allow it to rapidly explore a solar system or cross short distances across a galaxy.

Tom and Linda got excited about that idea and added that what was needed was a way to replenish the fuel for the Hole cannon or they needed to come up with a more efficient conversion process.

The discussions between the two and H^3 went on endlessly. They agreed that they would focus on getting the Cosmos Odyssey through the first time and that once that was a proven capability they would work on the additional capabilities that would add the flexibility that they had been discussing.

Joe and Lydia arranged a meeting with the President to explain the name the team had chosen. They had a short meeting with her and were pleased that she thought the choice was better than her suggestion. She asked Joe how that name was chosen and smiled when he said that it had been done in a very democratic way and the entire team had voted on seven name choices, one that included calling the ship the McAdam. He smiled and said that she came in a distant third in the voting but came in number one as the first guest passenger when she was ready.

Lacey laughed as she said that she would not need to worry about any future elections and that she was looking forward to life after the Presidency. She wondered if there might be a role for her in the Hole project.

Lydia smiled and said that the role of Cosmos Ambassador had not yet been filled and that she was sure that there would soon be the need for such a role.

Lacey nodded and said that she would keep that in mind, stood up and said she was off to her next meeting.

Lydia invited her to come to the ranch any time and that Uncle Ted could not stop talking about his time in the White House kitchen.

The three walked out of the meeting. They were surrounded by the security detail and parted ways when they got to the first hallway. Joe and Lydia were led out one way and the President went on down the hallway. Their normal guards were waiting for them when they came out to where the cars were parked.

Lydia asked whether they could walk over to the Lincoln Memorial and then walk to the other end of the Mall and back before they left Washington.

Joe suggested they do that and then have lunch at the Brazilian Churrascaria they had all talked about and see if it could match the steak they were used to getting at the ranch.

Their two Marine guards laughed and said that beating Uncle Ted's steaks would be hard to do but they were eager to check it out.

The four of them stopped at the Lincoln Memorial where they all agreed that it always caused them to pause and think about the mixed history that the US had. On the one hand it had a Declaration of Independence that highlighted liberty and justice for all but had embraced slavery in its early years because the people at the time did not consider their slaves as people but as property. That history had survived more than one hundred years and the biases between the races still existed and recently its ugly face had once again surfaced. The tension between the races still had an uncomfortable relationship if not a hateful race bias relationship.

The four knew immediately that they were the center of attention when they waited to be seated at the Brazilian Churrascaria. Lydia commented that they needed to get permission to have their guards wear civilian clothes versus the formal Marine uniform.

When free drinks were offered by the waiter for anyone at the table who was in the service their two guards smiled and said there was a benefit to wearing the uniform.

Joe nodded and said that he would prefer not to attract attention and would buy the drinks next time.

Not long after, Lydia turned her order card to the red side to signal that she had enough. She commented that the meat, the variety, its flavor, and the quantity was delicious, and it also included chicken, lamb, goat, and it seemed to go through every cut of beef.

Joe said that the meat was not necessarily better but it all tasted very good and the variety was exceptional.

The four of them walked out ready for their flight to Piñon Canyon. Lydia commented that she was glad that Jorge had lent them the use of the jet he used because there would be no waiting and they would be taking off immediately upon their arrival for the four hour flight. She shared that she planned to get a long nap in so that she would be ready to do some walking before they all met with the retrieval team that they would be working with.

Joe added that he was going to follow her lead and do the same. He suggested that their guards do the same as they all boarded the jet.

Upon their arrival at the Piñon Canyon facility landing strip, they were met by two army sergeants that let them know that they were to take them to their quarters and afterwards they were all expected at a dinner meeting at a new restaurant that was about a twenty minute drive away.

Lydia thanked the sergeant for the information and said that she would be ready in about thirty minutes. She asked what the dress code might be and was pleased to hear it was western casual. She had no idea what the meant but the word casual was all she needed to hear.

It turned out that Colonel Sanderson was using their arrival as a means to hold a celebration for his staff and the retrieval team. He was hoping that being part of the experiment would give him good exposure and lead to a promotion. He stood up and welcomed them and made the point that Joe and Lydia had just come from talking with the President and he was sure that the President had sent some encouraging words.

Lydia whispered to Joe that he was up to bat and she expected him to have learned something from Uncle Ted's story telling. It did not escape her that she was the one seated next to the Colonel and Joe was seated at the other end of the table.

Joe smiled as he stood up, slowly looked around and then began by saying that President Lacey had told him to let them know that because of the great people like them she felt sure that the United States would be the first nation to enjoy going out to the Cosmos. She had commented that the work that everyone was doing was like an Odyssey to be traveled and enjoyed. They would ensure that the effort would go from a fourteen foot hole in the Piñon Canyon to the galaxies beyond. In fact, she had authorized him to share with them the name of the spaceship that would make that journey. He stopped and looked around again. Then asked if anyone was interested to know that name?

Then everyone stood up and shouted that they wanted to know.

Joe laughed and said he thought so. He then said that the ship that would make the first transit to some distant galaxy would be the "Cosmos Odyssey." He then asked everyone to repeat it. Once the silence returned, he then looked very serious and said that they were among the first to know and that the name should be kept secret until they heard the President officially announce it or he would be fired and he needed his job to feed his ever growing family.

The base commander stood up and put his finger to his lips and quietly said that silence it was. He then said that dinner would be self-help and would go by the number on each table. He pointed at Joe and said that he was sitting at table number one. He then took Lydia's hand and said that he would escort her through the line.

Lydia mentally shook her head and wondered how the women on the base were able to handle him. It was all she could do not to pull her had away and she was glad when she was given her plate.

Six the next morning Lydia and Joe arrived at the Piñon Canyon room that was the command center. They had enjoyed the evening event and had returned to their quarters pleased by the importance that the base commander had given to the Hole effort. They had wondered what had made him so supportive and some casual discussion with the two sergeants that were escorting them let them know that the commander's assignment was almost up and the two were sure he was hoping for a more visible and higher profile next assignment.

Lydia asked if the commander deserved a promotion and a better assignment. She watched as the two looked at each other. It was clear to her that the Sergeant in the passenger seat did not want to say anything. The sergeant behind the wheel just shook his head in the negative and replied that neither of them would care to give a reply. Lydia knew the answer to her question but had no idea why. She decided that the way the two escorts had declined to answer was something that she would want to find out.

After their arrival, she quietly ask what they should do about the commander. Joe had suggested they pass the information to Jorge and then step away from it. He added that they had to keep their focus on the project. She agreed and squeezed his hand as they walked into the meeting room.

The entire retrieval team was present and had already started the checks on the equipment and retrieval team placement. The communications tech let everyone know that she was connected with Hole generation team in Lakland.

Jorge was sitting in his office. There were several screens, one of which was of the retrieval site. He kept having to keep himself from calling the Hole generation site the launch site. He and Jerry had discussed how hard it was to change their antiquated language. The difference to this test was that two cameras, radar and infrared sensors would go through the Hole first, and there would be a fraction of a second as they reported an all clear signal back before the model was sent through the Hole.

Tom, Linda, and H^3 were the only ones at the Hole generation site. They had spent the last hour with Arron inspecting the physical hardware. They all agreed that the increase in the size of the cabling was robust enough to handle the current that would surge through them. They had also agreed that the blast area was now over designed but that was not a significant issue.

The three of them had spent the previous day's reviewing the lead to energy transformation equations and had reached agreement that the refinements they had made were as accurate as current technology allowed them to be.

H^3 had been given the honor of being the test spokesman. He knew that Linda and Tom were recognizing him for his contribution. The impressive bright green six inch diameter Hole Generation button was located immediately in front of him. He smiled as he realized the hand he was extending to press the button was shaking and he found that his voice was shaky.

Lydia could see H^3's hand slowly going toward the button and knew that he was nervous. The camera panned on Linda and Tom and she thought about their development of the technology that had given her a new life.

H^3 pressed the button and two drones appeared at the designated Hole target site.

Lydia unconsciously shouted out, "we have two mice" and immediately after that the Model of the Cosmos Odyssey appeared and she shouted out that she had the mouse.

Jorge listened as everyone shouted out Lydia has the mouse.

Linda had tears in her eyes as she realized that Lydia had remembered her refrain that she had uttered after every successful test when she had been on the receiving end of the transmissions through the Door. Lydia had been the first human to have made that transition and she had heard herself being referred to as "the mouse."

Lydia and Joe recorded the fact that the three objects that had appeared at the receiving location had not fallen to the ground but remained hovering until the power at the Lakland end was turned off. They recorded this so that its significance could be evaluated. They also recorded the exact location of each of the objects appearance. They retrieved the three objects and immediately headed for their plane.

Tom, Linda, H^3 and the rest of the team gathered at the Hole generation site and inspected all the equipment. The energy transformation power lines were hot but within the range they had estimated they would be.

Only the first layer of the blast shield was impacted. This was reassuring to H^3 since he was the one that had greatly decreased the amount of lead to be transformed into energy.

They then focused on the accuracy of their calculations and were pleased that they had achieved a placement that exactly matched their calculations. Linda commented that they had hit the bullseye exactly dead center.

Tom commented that he wanted to repeat the test two more times to verify that they had a system that was dead accurate.

Jorge agreed to doing that but suggested that they do it in the next two days. Everyone agreed.

Ryan asked whether he should adjust the time for the actual launch of the Cosmos Odyssey.

Jorge asked him to work with the White House to set the date for the name change ceremony. The actual equipment needed to be mounted on the ship. He added when those two milestones were met they could set the launch date. He shook his head and asked if launch was the right term.

Joe commented that he was thinking of it as a launch since the Cosmos Odyssey would actually depart from the solar system. He asked whether a target had been selected.

Tom spoke up and said that he had been working with an astronomer that was assigned to General Delaney and they had been reviewing several systems that were within the Milky Way and several that were outside and at a much greater distance.

He and Linda were suggesting they select the closest location since it would give the team a way to further verify the current control system.

Jorge suggestion that the team agree to the closest location and save the more distant location for the next time got immediate agreement.

He called the meeting to an end and suggested that the test dates be set so Joe and Lydia could arrange to be at the receiving end.

9

<u>Ready….Set…. !</u>

The President had agreed to another meeting with her favorite General where she got an update on the progress of the Hole project. She complemented him on the accelerated schedule since it would give her administration another gold star that they would be able to boast about and would help her party to have a chance to stay in power. She agreed to the recommissioning ceremony date.

The last item that Jorge brought to her attention was the issue of the Piñon Canyon Facility commander. He let her know that he had no direct information but let her know that Lydia and Joe had discovered that there was something not quite right about the current situation. She agreed to have it checked out.

Jorge left the White House energized by the President's support for the project and relieved that he was no longer in the loop about the Piñon Canyon Facility commander's behavior. He was sure that it would not go well for the Commander. He trusted Lydia and Joe's assessment that there was something off with the Colonel's behavior.

Ryan had kept close track of the work going on up on the Cosmos Odyssey. He worked closely with Darian and Samantha who had the responsibility to do the physical inspections of the Hole generation cannon and the six mounted lead conversion thrusters that would push the Odyssey through the Hole. He and Aaron were doing the physical inspection of the six drones that would be the scouts that would verify the target area was clear of debris. Each of the drones had been augmented to include debris clearance lasers that would eliminate any small particles that might be in the target area space. This improvement had been suggested by Joe who had commented that the target zone at Piñon Canyon had dust blowing across from the winds in the area.

H^3 was completing the programming of the lasers that had been added to each of the six drones that would go through the hole first to ensure the area that was to be occupied by the Cosmos Odyssey was clear of even the smallest particles. He had reacted immediately to Joe's dust observation and had inspected the two drones and the model of the Cosmos Odyssey on each of the three tests. He had found the dust imbedded in the structure of the models. This sent an alarm bell through him as he realized that the structures going through the hole must actually assemble from the original location and reassemble at the destination location. When he shared this with Tom and Linda, they both commented that the transit through the Hole was different than they had imagined and they needed to continue to study and learn what was happening.

Joe listened to their worry and asked if the way they were sending the drones and the model of the Cosmos Odyssey wasn't the same methodology that they had used to transmit Darian, he and Lydia using the matter transmitter?

Tom shook his head and commented that there were many similarities but they had no way to reconstitute at the target end since they did not have a receiver so they had created the Hole to enable sending objects through.

Joe nodded and asked how they were sending the objects through.

Linda responded that they were using lead energy transformation engines to push the object through the hole.

Joe nodded again and asked how they were able to push a physical object through the hole without any resistance.

H^3 responded that Joe seemed to be hitting on a key point that might have been missed. Maybe the transition speed of the object actually separated the individual atoms of the object and then pulled them back together again at the destination and that was how dust particles could end up embedded in the structure of both the drones and the model.

Tom looked at Linda and asked if she agreed with H^3.

She shook her head and admitted that H^3 was operating at a level one step beyond her capability and the three of them should sit down and have H^3 explain each part of his transformation equation to see if the review would shed more light on what was happening during the transit through the Hole.

Jorge had listened to the exchange and suggested a review meeting where H^3 explained each piece of the transformation equation and what he thought was physically happening. Then anyone on the team could ask a clarifying question. He asked Lydia to be the person to facilitate the meeting and keep it focused on getting through the equation explanation and prevent circular discussions.

He asked H^3 to write down the equation on a series of white boards that would highlight what each portion of the equation did.

H^3 shook his head and said that he would need a series of boards and it would likely take a few days to set everything up.

Yara spoke up and said she would work with H^3 to get everything ready. She added that she would get each board ready and write out the equation so everyone could read each portion of the equation. She finished by saying that H^3's writing was illegible and he should have become a doctor.

Two days later when the team entered the meeting room three sides had white boards that were numbered one through twelve. Yara suggested that Joe and Lydia sit at the head of the table nearest the entry. Lydia would make sure that before moving from one board to another one all questions that had been asked was written down and that Joe agreed to moving on.

Lydia stood at her place at the head of the table and began by saying that she was agreeing to facilitate the meeting but she wanted to first complement and thank Tom, Linda, and H^3 for having given the team the gift of becoming travelers among stars.

She felt the team had an opportunity to contribute to the mathematics and physics that was well beyond their capabilities and she hoped the questions that they asked would help the three geniuses in refining the Hole and transfer equations so none of them would end up with dust particles embedded in their bodies.

The last part of her introduction got a loud, "Hurrah" from everyone in the room.

The review went smoothly until they reached board number seven. It was then Joe asked how the actual object transition happened. He listened intently and then asked how H^3 was getting the object to go through the Hole and that it seemed that the object could not leave its current location without some sort of instantaneous dissolution and then reconstitution.

H^3 was on his third attempt in his explanation when he stop and approached the section of the equation that was on the board.

Linda had been following the question. Then H^3's explanation. She walked up to H^3 and whispered in his ear.

H^3 looked at her, smiled and said that she did understand the math as well as he did and she was right. He pointed at the board and said that there was an anomaly that would cause the atoms of the object to spread and then come back together. He looked at Joe and asked him what made him ask the question.

Joe smiled and said that it was due to his cattle herding days when the herd would seemingly spread out for no reason and then immediately after they would come back together and continue to slowly go along the path that the lead cow was taking.

Joe's answer brought laughter to the room.

He looked around and said that was how cattle acted and maybe neutrinos and other atomic particles were more like a herd of cows than H^3 had thought.

H^3 smiled and said that he would come out to the Ranch and go observe the cattle to get a better handle on his math.

Jorge suggested that they take a break and then continue afterwards. During the break Tom asked him to authorize one more test before having the launch of the Cosmos Odyssey. Jorge asked about Tom's objective. He was surprised to learn that Tom had a way to measure the expansion to ensure that it would not affect a person. When he asked how he was going to do that. Tom smiled and said that he had a special mouse that he was going to put at risk. Jorge smiled, knew he wanted to see the mouse go through the hole. He agreed to the test.

Two days later, Lydia, Joe and Linda were at the Piñon Canyon facility. They were surrounded by the team they had been working with and the new site woman commander who greeted them.

The change did not escape Lydia. She wondered where Colonel Sanderson had ended up.

When the test took place, two scout drones came through and then a mouse came into view.

Linda smiled and shouted out, "I have a mouse." When the mouse was brought to her in a cage she reached in and let it curl up in her hand. She gave it a small crumb of cheese and said that she was going to give it an immediate CAT scan to see if it had any stray dust particles or any other problems.

Lydia nodded and said that having the mouse come through with seemingly no problems was very reassuring. She hoped that the CAT scan would not find any dust particles.

H^3 was pleased with the test and confided in Yara that he had refined his equation in several points and felt great about the review. He commented that Joe might not be a math whiz but he had an uncommon capability to ask questions that led to an improvement and he always seemed do things that helped the team improve.

Yara nodded in agreement and said that was why he continued to be the leader of the team.

Jorge listened to the learnings from the latest test. It seemed to him that the team was ready and that it was time to set the final schedule. He got Ryan to call a final plan review.

Ryan reviewed the bottle neck plan and pointed to the test of the Hole generation cannon, the firing of the six through the hole scout propulsion rockets and the formal commissioning of the Cosmos Odyssey by the President as the three events that were scheduled in sequence before the actual creation of the Hole by the Cosmos Hole generator. He pointed out that the only item that did not have a date set was the commissioning event which depended on the President's schedule.

Jorge said that he would contact the President and get her to set the date for the renaming event.

H^3 put up his hand and agreed to lead the Hole generation and the checkout of the six propulsion rockets if Joe would agree to participate in checking them out with him.

Joe smiled and asked when H^3 wanted to get that done.

Yara spoke up and said that they should work backward from the time the President would be available for the commissioning. The team making the journey should be on board the Cosmos Odyssey and after the renaming ceremony they should spend a couple of days discussing the journey and then create the Hole and GO.

Tom and Linda looked at each other and then Linda spoke up and said that she and Tom would like to on the team that took the first journey. They not only wanted to be among the first to travel to a distant galaxy but if there were any issues their presence might be useful. It would also give them additional information for any possible improvements.

Jorge could see that the team was ready to go. He looked around and realized that once again the first three humans to successfully verify the power of the Door would be among the first to also go to another galaxy. He hoped to be a part of the second trip when he, Jerry and the President would be among those going.

10

<u>Revenge</u>

Colonel Sanderson walked out of his performance review with his Major General boss. He had a bitter taste in his mouth and knew his career was toast. He had hoped that his performance at managing the Piñon Canyon Facility and his recent interactions with the secret Hole program would put him on track for a promotion. He instead was told that currently there were no assignments available and in a not too subtle way was given the suggestion he should consider resigning. When he inquired about the suggestion he learned that the suggestion had come down from the very top.

He left the meeting determined to find out who at the top would be making such a suggestion. He put out feelers about who at the top had make such a suggestion. He found it extremely hard to get the information but his perseverance yielded a surprise. He discovered the top meant the very top and that the President herself had put in motion a review of his behavior and how he was seen by the people he commanded. He then found out that people both in the military and in his social circles had given him reviews that bordered on being spiteful and hateful. He was furious and refused to interact with anyone at the facility.

10 Revenge

The more he thought about it he realized that his interaction with the people associated with the Hole project had to be the ones that had somehow and for some reason communicated this hateful information to the President.

His career was over.

His wife had initiated divorce proceedings on grounds of incompatibility.

He was devastated. Emotionally he was a wreck. Everything he had worked for had gone up in smoke because of spiteful people.

All he could think about was revenge. Revenge that would rub the noses of those malicious, horrible, superior people into the dirt. He wanted his revenge action to be a major event. One that left dozens of people dead.

He was willing to risk his life. He was prepared for that event, if he could take out the two who had come to his base and then pissed on his reputation with lies. He also wanted to do the same with the President but he didn't see a way that he could get close enough to her to take her out.

He set out on a mission to find out how to extract the revenge he desired.

He had several acquaintances at the Lakland base. He decided that it was time to rekindle and work those connections. He spent a month wining and dining them and learning about what was going on at Lakland.

He was surprised to learn that there was going to be a ceremony to rename a spaceship and that the Hole project was about another breakthrough in opening up space and that what he had witnessed was the experiments that would allow a full sized spaceship to instantly cross millions of miles of space.

He wondered whether it was real or only propaganda that would be used as political fodder for the next election. He really distrusted the political system and he certainly hated the fact that a woman had been elected President. He was certain that there was no way to break the fact that the speed of light was the fastest that anyone could travel through space. So, he concluded it was all a show for the camera and the people watching.

What caught his attention was that the President would personally lead the renaming ceremony and be present for the first launch. He used his remaining time as the Piñon Canyon Commander to wrangle an invite to the ceremony. He would leverage that invite to not only disrupt the event but to make worldwide history when he assassinated the President of the United States.

The day after he had arranged everything he got word that he had been replaced by a female Lieutenant Colonel. He was furious at the insult that had been thrown at him by his commanding officer. Not only was a woman replacing him but one that was one rank below him. It was a double kick in the gut.

He was able to wrangle a helicopter ride to Lakland the day before he was to transition his command. He was not going to be present when command transition happened. He figured not being present would send a clear way of making his last statement about having a woman replace him.

He flew to Lakland by helicopter and accepted a room at the base officer's residential facility. He was several days early but figured he would keep to his room and keep a low profile.

He had his favorite bolt action ten round 308 in a carrying case that looked like a guitar case. He planned to take out the entire contingent that would most likely be up on a speaking platform. He hoped to fire ten rounds reload and continue to mow down everyone on the platform. He was sure the surprise attack on the base would be so disruptive that the response would be slow enough for him to slaughter a bunch of the snobs.

Afterwards he would give himself up and face the music. He was sure he would face the death penalty but he figured he would be on death row for years as his lawyers appealed the death penalty.

He donned jogging clothes and went to where the ceremony was to be held and checked out the lay of the land. He was pleased with the way the hill side sloped up to a semicircle row of big old maple trees. He found a spot up in the largest of the trees where he could sit unseen. He returned to his room and spent time cleaning his weapon and wiping each bullet as if each was a precious piece of gold jewelry.

Lydia was sitting in the same couch where she had spent the night before she was to be transported the first time through the Door. She was looking at the renaming event guest list. It was clear to her that the President had invited some key political personalities. She was surprised that the President had selected members from both parties but she figured it was part of the Presidents strategy.

She glanced over to where Joe was sitting in the chair that he had sat in that eventful night before her transport through the Door. That was the night before the miraculous transformation that had occurred and it was the night she now looked back on as the night she had fallen in love with him. That feeling was sealed the next day when Joe was sitting outside of the transit receive room when she was led out to be taken to the hospital. She had surprised herself when she leaned over and had given him a kiss and thanked him for being there the night before.

She refocused on the renaming invitation list that she was holding.

"Joe who do you think invited Colonel Sanderson to this event," she asked?

Joe looked up from the book he was reading, shook his head, and replied that he had no clue but it was likely because he was the Piñon Canyon Commander.

"I hope he gets a seat in the far back," Lydia responded.

The next day Lydia asked around about the invitation and could not find anyone who knew how he had been invited.

She and Joe made several transits up to the Cosmos Odyssey to familiarize themselves with the modified control panel and the new seating arrangement in the control center.

She would be sitting directly behind Joe. Darian would sit to Joe's left and Samantha sat behind him. H^3 would sit to the right of Joe and Yara sat behind him.

The back row was raised so they could look down at the main control panel and know the condition of the ship. Tom and Linda's seats were located to the left and right of the back row.

She joked that if they hit a wall the front row would save the beauties in the back row.

Joe asked if she wanted to have the seating arrangement changed.

She shook her head and said the layout worked well and she was satisfied.

Joe had the entire team come up together to rehearse several times until he felt they were ready for the upcoming journey to some distant galaxy.

The day of the renaming ceremony arrived. Joe and Lydia were among the first to arrive at the presentation venue. They took in the layout for the event. The stage faced North toward the Hole test site that was visible through the ring of large Maple trees that created a border around the field where the event was staged.

The speaker's podium was to the right of where Joe and Lydia and the rest of the team would be sitting. The top Hole program leadership, the President and those she had invited would be sitting to the right of the podium. The security personnel would stand to the sides and rear of the raised stage area.

Early in the wee hours of the morning while it was still dark, Colonel Sanderson had made his way to the tree he had chosen to use. He climbed up to where a limb provided a place for him to sit out of view from the stage but give him a good position to fire his rifle. He had dressed in camouflage so that it was almost impossible to see him. He made himself comfortable and as the daylight slowly crept in he made sure he had a good view of the stage and the podium and that he was indeed not easily spotted. He looked through the scope to make sure he had a clear view. He cleared away a few small branches. He watched as several airmen wiped the dew from the chairs and got everything ready. He enjoyed the music that was being used to test the sound system and almost laughed when one of the airmen began to sing.

The Hole team members minus Tom and Linda who were to sit to the left of the podium were the first to arrive and take their seats. The audience made up mostly of the base's personnel augmented by a large team of Marines that worked for General Delaney were all seated when the band located to the center back played Hail to the Chief as the President walked up on the stage. She was followed by General Martinez and General Delaney. Linda and Tom followed after the Generals.

Colonel Sanderson had to contain himself to wait for the ideal time for his revenge. He kept looking around the trunk of the tree to locate the people he planned to shoot first. For the first time in weeks, he felt that he was in command.

Jorge walked up to the podium waved his left hand over to where Joe and the team sat and then out to the audience. He made the comment that it was a very special day. They were all there to officially launch the Hole program that had been made possible by the geniuses, H^3, Linda and Tom . He stopped and asked the three to stand up. He then added that they and the team to his left was going to give the United States a giant lead in world leadership.

He went on to say that it was his honor and pleasure to have the President of the United States come to speak to all of them and to officially name the spaceship that would take the team to his left to some galaxy billion of miles away.

The colonel knew that the moment to take his shot was about to happen. He took a deep breath as he realized he was shaking in anticipation. He took a moment to look through his scope at the three he planned to shoot. He watched the General bow slightly as he introduced the President by saying, "Let me yield the podium to President Lacey McAdam.

Just before the President stood up and Jorge stepped toward her, Joe saw a red spot on Lydia's chest. He stood, kicked her chair hard enough to the side that the whole row of chairs and the people in them fell over like a row of dominos.

He looked out to the trees and saw a glimmer of light flash in the largest of the maple trees. He did not hesitate but ran at what seemed to him to be slow motion, full speed toward the podium, grabbed President McAdam, turned with her in his arms so she was behind him and then pushed her backward down to the platform floor.

He felt the bullet hit him in his left shoulder. He rolled, got up and ran to the edge of the stage, took Sergeant Stanley's scoped 308, turned to where he had seen the glint in the tree and fired without trying to aim. Then he took the time to look through the scope and saw the person looking through the scope of a rifle back at him. This time he fired at the center of the scope and watched as the rifle was dropped and someone fell out of the tree. He jumped down from the stage and sprinted toward the tree. He was followed by a number of armed airmen and a contingent of the President's guards.

Up in the tree the Colonel watched as the whole row of people seemed to fall across the stage. He had been about to shoot the bitch that had embarrassed him by ignoring him. He was amazed at the speed of the snobby guy racing toward the President. Things were moving faster than he could think. He had planned to first shoot the two who he was sure had been the cause of being relieved of his command. His rifle followed that person running toward the President and at the last moment he decided to shoot her but he was too late. His shot hit the person; he recalled as Joe in the back. He was surprised when Joe, who he had just shot ran to the edge of the stage took a rifle out of the hands of the Marine standing there and fired it.

He ducked behind the tree as the bullet took out the bark near where he was sitting. He looked through his scope and was about to fire when the world went black.

Joe stood looking down at the person on the ground. Half of the Colonel's face was blown away by the bullet he had fired at him but Joe was able to recognize that it was Colonel Sanderson the Piñon Canyon Commander.

He felt someone's hand on his shoulder, looked up and realized that it was General Delaney.

The General said, "Once again you are the hero of the moment. Let's get your wound looked at before you bleed to death."

It was then that Joe realized that blood was dripping from his left hand. He handed Sergeant Stanley's rifle back to him as he walked over to where the EMT's guided him. The next few moments were very confusing as the medics took off his suit jacket, cut off his shirt and then stopped the bleeding and hauled him away in an ambulance. He lost track of what was happening.

He was just getting out of having the wound sewn shut and bandaged when a contingent of black suited men entered and President McAdam came in. She came over and gave him a gentle hug. She then stepped back and said that she was going to give him a medal of honor for his bravery. She added that he now was not only her favorite of the Fold and the Hole team but the person that she would forever think about on a daily basis as the person who had indeed taken a bullet for her.

She let out a laugh and said that at least she would do all that after she got over the bruise she was going to have on her butt from having been tackled and thrown down by him. She asked him if he would be ready by that afternoon for a continuation of the ceremony.

Joe smiled and said that he was willing to do that immediately but he no longer had a suit to wear.

Lacey looked around and asked that whoever wore the same size suit should please get it dry cleaned and let Joe wear it.

As the men in black escorted the President out, Lydia walked in and gave Joe a hug. She had been crying from the emotion of having watched the entire scene of Joe tackling the President and seeing the bullet hit and go through his shoulder. She had stood up from where Joe had pushed her chair and knocked over the entire row. For some reason, her eyes glued in on the spot where the bullet had hit and embedded itself in the platform. She had then looked over to where Joe had taken a rifle from Jeff their Marine body guard and fired twice before jumping up and running full speed toward the back of the crowd. She had noted that the Jeff had his pistol drawn as he followed and that a dozen armed persons were also running after Joe, but they were a good twenty feet behind him. She knew that if the shooter was still alive, Joe had put himself in mortal danger.

She looked at Joe and said that not only did she love him but she thought he was a little crazy and she loved that part too.

General Martinez walked in, smiled, and said, "fools rush in where Angels fear to tread." He then came to where Joe was sitting and gave him a salute and said that he had never seen anyone act more decisively or more deadly than he had just witnessed. He added that General Delaney told him that he once again was the hero of the moment and had prevented the assassination of the President.

Joe smiled and asked if that meant that he could have an extra desert at the evening's celebration.

Jorge laughed and nodded and said he could also have an extra anything else that he might want. He then asked if he had agreed to be present at the ceremony that would take place in an hour.

Lydia looked at the clock and realized that almost three hours had passed since the assassination attempt.

Joe said that he could make it but he had a couple of things he needed to do before then.

11

<u>Ceremony and Vacation</u>

Joe called Tom and asked if he would transport him to the Cosmos Odyssey a couple of times.

Tom looked at him and then smiled. He nodded and said he would be very honored to do so.

When Tom got to the transmit room he was surprised to find the President standing in a white robe with two female FBI guards. Joe was standing in a white robe as well. He said that both he and the President would make the transport to the ship and then after giving her a tour they would both transport back.

Tom nodded and waved to the entrance to the transmit chamber.

Joe went in first. He threw his robe out and stood on the footprints that were the transmit position. He arrived on the Cosmos Odyssey, got dressed and put out the clothes for the President. He then went to the control room area to wait.

A few moment later the President walked into the Cosmos Odyssey control room. She smiled and commented that she now understood why he was the one that everyone looked to in an emergency. She smiled and commented that after the transport her bruises were gone and she would be able to sit down without the pain.

After a quick tour, Joe made sure that the President knew how to make the return trip through the Door and then went first.

A few moments later the President made the trip back to the Door located in the Lakland Door center.

Not long after, Joe was back on stage in a freshly laundered black suit. His shoulder was healed and the suit was now a little oversized since it was a couple of sizes bigger than he normally wore. He was wearing the black sunglasses that he had persuaded the presidential body guard, who had brought him the suit, to let him use. Except that he was thinner than all the President's bodyguards, he looked almost exactly like the rest of them. He was sitting next to Lydia who was now in a black off shoulder dress accented by a white one inch stripe that ran from arm to arm across her chest and white strips that ran down both sides of the dress to its bottom hem that just touched the floor. It was clear to him that she had chosen that dress because of his black suit. All he could think about was that she was more beautiful than ever.

President McAdam came to the stand and made a point of introducing the man in black, Joe Elsinger, the body guard who had taken a bullet for her. She asked Joe to stand. Joe took Lydia's hand and pulled her up to stand beside him. He then turned and swept his left hand to recognize the rest of the team. There was a moment of silence then everyone in the audience clapped and all the Marines let out a loud "Orah." Joe raised Lydia's hand with his, nodded and sat back down with a noticeable red face. He was glad that he was wearing the dark sunglasses.

Lydia knew that Joe found it hard to accept public praise. She gave his hand a squeeze. She was pleased with how he had handled the situation by including the rest of the team.

President McAdam launched into her prepared speech about the upcoming journey that the Hole team was about to go on. She described Doorship One that had been Captained by Joe and his team and had delivered the first Doors out into the Solar System. Those Doors opened the Solar System to the US and some key participants that had supported the Door effort. She went on to comment that the ship was of a unique Brazilian ceramic design. It had recently been modified to house the Hole generation equipment at the center of the six sided wheel and had six through the hole transport thrusters mounted at the junctures of the six wheel sections. She pointed once again at Joe and said that the person who had saved her, Joe Elsinger was being promoted to the position of Admiral of the Space Corps. She held up a single piece of paper, accepted a pen from one of her guards and as she signed the paper she said that she was officially changing the name of Doorship One to USS Cosmos Odyssey. It would be the first of many starships that she was sure would follow. She then emphasized that Admiral Joe Elsinger would be in command of the USS Cosmos Odyssey. He was to have, Captain Lydia Tabata and Technical Specialist Captain H^3 reporting to him as well as the rest of the Hole team.

Tom stood up and shout, "Hurrah for Admiral Joe,   Hurrah for Admiral Joe."

This caused the President to turn to her right, point to Tom and then loudly shout, "Hurrah for Admiral Joe."

The audience and the rest of those on staged joined in and the Hurrahs continued for at least five minutes.

President McAdam walked over to Joe and handed him the certificate that renamed the Doorship and shook his hand. She quietly once again thanked him and said that on an Admiral's pay he should easily be able to afford the vacation she was ordering him to take before the Cosmos went through the Hole.

Joe accepted the certificate, nodded, and replied that a vacation was what he needed. He gave her a salute and said that he would follow her orders.

The presentation ended and both the President and Joe were surrounded by well-wishers and those wanting to shake their hands. It was an hour before they were on the way to the smaller gathering that was in Jorge's backyard.

Uncle Ted and his father Trey were both in attendance. His father came over to him and commented that they had waited until the smaller reception before congratulating him. His father looked at Joe and quietly commented that Joe had made his mother very proud and she was celebrating the fact that he had reached the rank of Admiral in one giant leap. He went on to say that he had been in the front row and had watched him in action. He added that he knew the instant that he stood up that something bad was about to happen. What happened was so fast that it had taken him and Ted the rest of the day to absorb it all.

Joe laughed when Uncle Ted said that he could not make up a story that would top what Joe had done that day. Uncle Ted added that all those hours target practicing had paid off. Joe nodded and said that his actions had all been reactions to the situation he found himself in. He didn't have time to think and his body did what it had learned to do and it did it on its own. He gave both Uncle Ted and his Father a hug and quietly thanked them for having been such great parents.

Joe had taken the time to change out of the black suit, He was dressed in blue jeans and a blue and white Kennebunk sports shirt. He felt much more relaxed then when he had on the black suit. He had thanked the men in black for lending him the suit but let them know that he was really much happier in his normal clothes.

Lydia had a similar outfit to his but her yellow and white blouse seemed to Joe to radiate her beauty much like a yellow rose highlighted by a sun beam.

She came over with a grilled rib steak, grilled asparagus and a baked potato and an empty plate. She led the way to a table and put everything down. She knew that Uncle Ted had prepared the beef that was being grilled and after her first bite she commented that he had out done himself and it was the best steak that she had ever tasted.

Uncle Ted thanked Lydia, gave her a hug, and then said that he had prepared the same steak that he had served the General and the President when the General had come to let her know that her suggestion of renaming Doorship One to Starship One had lost out to Cosmos Odyssey.

He laughed and said that he was sure that it was the steak that made the difference in the President accepting the fact that her suggestion had come in fourth out of five possible names.

Lacey had changed into a casual dark camel striped long sleeve t-shirt and jeans. She was standing behind Uncle Ted with a steak and asparagus on her plate. As she took a seat next to Lydia she added that the President had loved the steak but she was a person who believed in the democratic process and the fact that her entrance was fourth on the list was an indication that democracy worked.

Uncle Ted turned looked at her and let out a whistle. He added that she was the most beautiful President that he had ever voted for.

Lacey smiled and said that she was going to have the Hemphill County voting records checked to make sure he had voted for her in the last election because she had lost the state of Texas.

Tom and Linda came to their table and they both gave a toast before going back to the table where they were sitting with H^3, Yara, Darian, and Samantha.

Jorge and Jimena came over with their plates. Jorge asked whether a lowly General might be granted permission to sit with a President and an Admiral.

Joe's father smiled and patted the seat beside him and said that Admiral or President in his eyes everyone at the table had equal status.

The next day the entire team boarded the jet made available to take them to Maui on vacation. This time they were going to the Island that Lydia had wanted to go on her honeymoon but had been rerouted to Kuai because of the threat to their lives. The two guards that had accompanied them to Kuai were going to Maui with them. They let her know that they had done everything possible to make the trip with the team.

They landed in Maui and Lydia led the way to the tram over to the car rental building. She had arranged to have two vans to transport the team to the two B&B rentals that she had found. The one she had chosen featured a private beach and had enough room for half of them. The other was a three minute walk away and was a one minute walk away from a small beach. She suggested that their two guards split up and each choose one of the houses where they could stay.

Joe walked out between the two walls of black lava that led to the opening where he planned to swim. He was now thinking about trip through the Hole to some place in the Universe that Tom, Linda, and a team of astronomers were discussing. It seemed that they were concerned about both distance and the amount of debris that might be at the destination location. Joe knew that there was no way of knowing except to send the six scout ships through and have them check. He decided that he would suggest that they chose three destinations and let the crew of the Cosmos Odessey make the final selection.

He swam out a short distance from the black lava opening and looked back. The top deck of the house came into view and he saw Lydia standing and looking back at him. It was a moment that caught him by surprise. He waved to see if she could see him. He was pleased when she waved back. He watched as she turned and left the second floor. A few moments later he could see her walking out towards him. Her beauty always caught him by surprise and he once again thought about how lucky he was.

He took her hand and the two of them floated just holding hands and periodically giving each other a light kiss. He was really glad that they had taken the vacation.

12

<u>A New Scenario</u>

Tom and Linda had not accompanied the team on vacation. Instead, they were working and struggling to agree where the Cosmos Odyssey should go. They had reduced the list to three locations but could not agree which was the best choice. They had no clue how the choice would be made and decided follow Joe's suggestion to get the whole team to make the decision.

The team spent four days on Maui and then agreed that they had done all they wanted to do and thinking about their upcoming journey was keeping them from enjoying their time in paradise. They all agreed to return to Lakland and get the journey on the way.

Joe let Jorge know that the team was headed back and that they would expect to get on the way within a day or two.

Jorge arranged a meeting with Linda, Tom, and the lead astronomers they were working with.

At the meeting Linda summarized the situation as one where there was no way to choose which would be the best first target to send the team.

Jorge thought about the situation, smiled, and said that he was going to defer to their Admiral.

Tom smiled and said he agreed that the Admiral should make the choice.

The team landed at Lakland late in the afternoon and were informed that they were all invited to a backyard barbecue at the General's house.

Samantha laughed and said that she was sure that they were all walking into a mouse trap and they were the mice.

Lydia nodded and suggested they all go, enjoy the steaks, all the other goodies and let Joe taste the cheese to see what would happen.

Joe laughed and said that nothing was going to happen during the cook out. They should all relax because the action would happen the next day. He added that after the cookout he wanted them all to walk back to their quarters together because he wanted to share some ideas that he had.

Jorge was at the grill grilling steaks, brats, and sausages.

Tom and Linda led the way through the line and everyone grabbed a plate and followed.

Jimena was at the self-serve table making sure everyone got a plate with their choice of meat, mashed or baked potato, and grilled vegetables. She asked each of them how vacation had been as she put the food on their plates.

With Jerry, some of his team members and the eight bodyguards there were twenty eight people sitting at tables that were laid out in a hexagon. There was a barrel full of ice and a selection of soft drinks, beer, and wine at the joints between the tables.

Jorge walked to the center of the arrangement and lit the fire pit and welcomed the team that was making sure the Odessey would make a successful first journey.

Tom complemented Jorge on simulating the Cosmos Odessey in his back yard.

H^3 raised his bottle and made a toast, "may the Hole be large enough and the destination dust free."

Joe followed with, "may our scouts do their job and may the team make the journey a success."

The eating was constantly interrupted by ongoing toasts but everyone got plenty to eat and the night was the success that Jorge had hoped it would be. He watched the team relax and enjoy themselves and felt sure that they would once again pull off a journey full of surprises that would open up a new horizon for mankind.

Shortly after everyone had a chance to have desert, Joe stood up and said that he was calling it a night and heading back to his quarters.

12 A New Scenario

Jorge knew that something was up when all the team members stood up and said they were going as well. He reminded everyone that the meeting the next day would start at nine sharp. He watched as everyone leaving raised their hands and waved. He went over to where Tom and Linda were sitting and asked if they had any idea what the team was up to.

Tom shook his head and replied that he thought the Admiral would surprise them during the coming meeting.

Linda smiled and said she agreed that they would all most likely be surprised but she was ready to listen and most likely be one of the supporters of what they were about to hear.

On the way back to their quarters, Joe stopped and addressed the team. He then laid out what he was going to ask for at the morning meeting. He wanted to modify how they would make the transition to some distant galaxy. He wanted the sequence to include sending a Door through the hole first before the Cosmos Odessey went through. The Door would be modified to include a module where two people could stay. The Door would be moved to the edge of the area that the Cosmos Odessey would occupy. The Door would be tested by having a mouse sent to it and then retrieved. Then two of the team would go through the Door. Instead of the Cosmos Odessey coming through first, a four person module capable of both space and atmosphere flight would be sent through. The two team members that had transited via the Door would use the spacecraft to examine the area visually and telescopically. He went on to say that the spacecraft would be armed with a laser and a small, guided missile tube.

The two lead persons would then give the all clear. But before the Cosmos Odessey came through another set of six clearing drones would come through and in a slightly different configuration and verify that fact that the area that the Cosmos would occupy would be free of dust. To ensure that none of them had ended up with any dust particles in their bodies they would make a transition via the Door back to Earth and then back to the Cosmos Odessey via the Door on the Cosmos.

Darian laughed, said that Joe had been listening to too many of Uncle Ted's stories and then asked if Joe had anything of importance to share with the team other than an amazing bedtime story.

Samantha punched Darian on his shoulder and said that she was volunteering him to be the one that got Folded through first. She looked at Joe and said that she was volunteering to be one of the two people to go to through the Door first.

Lydia shook her head suggested that instead of sending anyone to an unarmed Door Module the first send through the clearance lasers followed by self-defense lasers and bring the Odessey through with the two attack craft ready to act but still attached to the a Odessey.

She then suggested that they should all get a good night's sleep so they would be able to keep from laughing when the Hole leadership team fell out of their seats upon hearing what Joe was about to propose.

She suggested they all meet for breakfast and get any questions that they might want answered before the meeting so they could be a team supporting any request that was put forward.

Yara nodded and added that she was sure that H^3 was going keep her awake most of the night as he digested what she and Joe had just proposed.

Tom and Linda had driven by the small park where the team had stopped. Linda commented that a meeting where Joe was convincing the team of what he had in mind and it was going to keep her up wondering what he had come up with. She added that she was glad that H^3 was part of that group.

Tom chuckled and said that he was going to get a very good night's sleep because he knew that Admiral Joe and his team would suggest very practical ideas that would eliminate their concern as which location to pick.

Jorge and Jerry were helping Jimena clean up the back yard. Jerry looked at Jorge and said that he had the feeling that in the morning the two of them would be listening to their Admiral share a new twist to the journey through the hole. He wondered what the President would say about what her Admiral was planning. He added that he did not think the Admiral would be asking permission but giving orders.

Jorge smiled and said that the two of them should be ready to salute and reply that they would do as ordered.

Jerry laughed and said that neither an Air Force or a Marine General was going to get in the way of their newly promoted Admiral.

Jemena had been listening to the banter and added that their Admiral was the reason that the project had reached the point where once again a new frontier was going to be opened. She was sure that Joe would suggest ideas that would greatly improve the outcome of the Hole program.

Lydia walked hand in hand the rest of the way to the house they shared with Darian and Samantha. Darian and Samantha were behind them. One of their guards walked in front of them and one behind them.

Lydia was making her point about her slant on what Joe was thinking.

Samantha asked when Joe had come up with what he had just shared.

Joe admitted that it had been during the flight back from Maui. He had not been able to sleep and it seemed that his mind would not quit coming up various scenarios.

This had kept up throughout the cook out and it was still brewing. He added that Lydia had really helped get things into a battel scenario fucus. He hoped that at breakfast there would be lots of questions from the team and that during the meeting more challenges or ideas would pop up. All he knew was that the team had to make sure that going through the Hole would be safe, that they could defend themselves and that they would all be able to return.

He also wanted the team to have some means to getting around the location where they found themselves in something other than their gigantic space wheel.

Darian asked if Joe would consider letting he and Samantha go through the Door to the location that he chose to make the trip through the Hole.

Joe laughed and said that he was only going to send a mouse through first and that he did not plan to send a pig before he sent a person.

Darian bowed his head and said that he now had great confidence in the Door technology and was willing to go after a mouse.

Lydia turned back and looked at Samantha and Darian and said that she certainly would let him go to a new universe ahead of her and that he was lucky to have such a brave partner who was willing to go with him but she was more worried about them being vulnerable to being attacked.

That night before she fell asleep, she gave Joe a hug and said that he was proving to come up with real life situations that out did any story that she had heard Uncle Ted tell.

Joe nodded and said that he was going to blame Uncle Ted for warping his mind. He wondered himself how he had come up with what he was going to insist on before the team made the journey through the Hole. He also wondered how much time it would take for their requests to be fulfilled.

The morning seemed to arrive almost immediately after he had fallen asleep. He took a hot shower and got dressed in the clothes he always wore at the ranch.

He and Lydia were the last to arrive for breakfast.

H^3 had the most questions. He wondered about the reason that a Door would be sent through first.

Joe replied that during the reconstruction process, the Door removed imperfections in a person's body. That would make sure that whoever came through would not have dust buried in them. The Door would also allow the team to send a sacrificial mouse to ensure that it was operating as desired. He added that the twelve versus just six dust elimination lasers would do a faster more thorough job before the gigantic Cosmos Odyssey arrived.

Lydia suggested that after the Odessey arrived everyone on board just transit to the door that was at the edge of the entrance globe and back to ensure they were dust free.

Joe looked around to the team and commented that he also had a concern about being attacked by beings that were terrified of being invaded by Aliens. So, he was having the two four person spacecrafts armed with a laser and a self-propelled rocket launcher. He added that he was not looking for a fight but he was going to be prepared to win if there was one.

Yara asked if he really thought they would meet beings that were advanced enough to have missiles that they would shoot at them.

Joe shook his head and said that he had no idea but he was going to follow the Boy Scout motto of, "Be Prepared."

Lydia pointed to her watch and said that it was time for them to get to Jorge's meeting.

12 A New Scenario

13

<u>Change in Plans</u>

Jorge noted that the team walked in together. He was sure that they had all been discussing whatever Joe had in mind. Joe had given him a heads up that there were some changes that he had in mind. This was something of a surprise because in their last conversation before the team's return from Maui, Joe had insisted that they go through the Hole in the next couple of days. He was very curious what had happened to make Joe change his mind.

He, however, wanted to begin the meeting with a surprise for Joe. The President had sent out the uniform that she had designed for the first Admiral of Interstellar Command, a new branch of the military. He welcomed everyone to the meeting and let them know that the President was still getting over the assassination attempt and she had sent out a gift for Joe. He held up the white uniform with gold shoulder boards that had four stars on them and said that it had been designed and tailored for Joe.

Joe walked up and accepted the uniform. He shook his head and said that he wondered when he would ever wear it. He felt that it was not appropriate for him to assume the rank since he had no actual military training other than the astronaut training they had all received. He thought it was an honor that he would accept but it would take a very special circumstance for him to wear the uniform of an Admiral.

He looked at Jorge and Jerry the two generals in the room and said that he had not had to maneuver up the ladder of command in any military to earn the distinction of being addressed as Admiral.

Tom laughed and said that uniform or no uniform, Joe had become recognized as the leader of the Hole project and he was eager to hear what he had in mind.

Joe looked at H^3 and asked for him to share the ideas that the team had discussed and wanted to get implemented before the Cosmos Odessey made its way through the Hole.

Jorge smiled and said that he thought, "the Admiral was referring to his flagship the USS Cosmos Odessey."

Joe nodded and pointed to H^3.

H^3 very accurately described what Joe had in mind, the reason, and the details of making it all happen.

Linda had been listening intently. When H^3 finished she said that everything that had presented was dead on.

These were details that had been over looked in the excitement of making the breakthrough and now that she had heard them she wondered how she and Tom could have missed such critical details and have missed levering the Door technology in such a positive manner. Delivering Doors to the distant galaxies ensured that future trips could easily take place.

Tom's face was red as he said that he probably had missed all those details because he had not killed nine hundred and ninety nine mice during the development of the Hole technology. He looked at H^3 and said that it was his fault for so rapidly doing all the deep thinking and developing such complicated equations. That brought a laugh from everyone in the room.

Darian gave his snide comment that good leaders always knew who to blame when things did not work out as they planned.

Jorge looked over at Ryan and asked him how long would it take to fulfill all of Joe's requests.

Ryan shook his head. He said that he could possibly get three doors that were getting built for hospitals repurposed to the Hole team. Having a live in module added to the Door could be accomplished relatively fast. He had no idea about the time it would take to get the two smaller four person fighter craft designed and built.

General Delaney volunteered that his team had such a craft. They had one ready to go and could have a second ready within a month. He added that the propulsion for both of them could be modified and the weaponry could be easily added.

Ryan looked around and said that he would put together a critical path schedule by that afternoon and let everyone know what the delay might be.

Darian spoke up and said he was not interested in a delay schedule but the date for his trip through the Hole so he would know when to stop his celebration drinking.

Joe looked at Darian and said that he would not be doing too much drinking because he was going to be working with Lydia to get the Doors and the attached living units certified good to go. He was to personally test each unit.

He pointed to H^3 and Yara and asked them to verify the propulsion for the four seater spaceships. It would be great to test them in the atmosphere and also out in space. Then they needed to be sent up and secured to the Cosmos.

He asked Tom and Linda to make sure that they had enough fuel and Door reconstitution materials to allow for all team members to make multiple trips through the Door and each of the four seat fighters that could make at least a dozen long trips.

Darian couldn't resist and loudly asked what the Admiral of Interstellar Command was planning to do?

Joe smiled and said the he was going to relax and throw back a couple with the Generals.

In reality Joe was scheduled to spend the following day getting interviewed and debriefed by two of the Army's Judge Advocates. They were doing the investigation into Colonel Sanderson's attempted assassination of the President.

They were interested in how Joe had been able to take such quick and decisive action when everyone else seemed to be frozen in place. They had commented that it seemed that he knew exactly what was going to happen.

He had mentioned that comment to Jorge. He added that he would find it hard to act coolly if accused of being part of the plot to assassinate the President.

Jorge said that he wanted to hear from him if the advocates implied any association of the Colonel with he or anyone on the team.

That afternoon when Joe walked into the meeting room, the two advocates went immediately to the relationship between Joe and Colonel Sanderson.

Joe looked at the two and asked if they were worried that he had shot his best friend out of the tree.

The senior advocate commented that Joe and the Colonel had met several times and the Colonel had thrown a celebration dinner for him. It seemed that the two had some sort of relationship.

Joe shook his head and let them know that the Colonel had used his and Lydia's trip as part of the Hole project as an excuse for the celebration dinner. He informed them that he and Lydia had arrived from a meeting with the President and the Colonel had taken the opportunity to say that the President had said good things about the folks at Piñon Canyon. He made the point that the President and he had never discussed Piñon Canyon but he had adlibbed some good words for her because the people at the gathering had all been part of two previous Hole project transmission events.

The younger advocate asked if Joe always adlibbed good words for the President.

Joe shook his head, smiled, and said that he seldom had the opportunity. He then looked at her and suggested that the questioning take a more positive approach or he would pull rank, leave the meeting, and ask that the Army Judge Advocate consider why the Colonel had lost his life and have the inquiry guided in a more appropriate direction. He added that he was not going to sit with the two of them and be accused of being involved in an assassination attempt.

There was a moment of silence, and the younger advocate apologized and said that she would focus on how the Colonel had received an invitation to the renaming event.

Joe nodded, said that he and Lydia had discussed that exact question and had not been able to find anyone that had invited him. He figured that he had wrangled the invite before his Piñon Canyon demotion had become known. He added that if they found out how he had been able to get into the base without being seen that information would be useful in improving base security.

The older JAG commented that the Colonel had arrived at Lakland on an Army helicopter. He evidently had brought his weapon with him. He had also arranged for a stay at the Lakland officers temporary quarters.

He explained that the Colonel had arrived two days early and had kept a low profile by staying in his room and ordering in food that was delivered to him.

Joe looked at him and asked if the two of them knew so much why was he being grilled versus just informed.

The older JAG nodded and said that they were looking for who had made the invite and they currently did not have a clue. They had acted the way they had because they were amazed at the speed with which he had reacted.

Joe shared that a red laser spot on Lydia's chest and the morning sun's reflection from the spot where the Colonel was located was the only warning that he had and his reaction was almost too slow. He commented that everything had gone into slow motion for him and everything he had done was done without thinking. He didn't even know he had been shot until General Delaney told him to let the EMT's check on is wound.

He then suggested that they look at the Lakland personnel records and look for the persons that had worked with the Colonel earlier in his career or had attended college with him.

The older JAG nodded and said that he would follow up on that suggestion. He went on and apologized about the line of questioning that the two of them had pursued.

Joe shook his head and said that no apology was necessary. What he really wanted to know was how the Colonel had been able to get on the base and who the people whether knowingly or by chance had facilitated it. He wanted that to be shared with Doug Hasterly the base security officer so that it could not happen again.

The advocate wondered whether Lydia would have any information about the Colonel.

Joe nodded in the affirmative and said that she was the one who the Colonel had seemed to focus on with some behavior she felt verged on it being inappropriate.

She had asked two army sergeants who had been assigned to drive them what they thought of the Colonel. They basically refused to give her a straight answer. She would likely know their names.

The older JAG nodded and said that they were scheduled to interview both General Jerald Delaney and General Jorge Martinez immediately after his interview and they would see when they could talk with Lydia.

Joe nodded, smiled, and added that both of them had several discussions with Colonel Sanderson. And it was General Martinez that had taken his and Lydia's concern about the Colonel's practices and behavior and shared it with the President. That information was the reason the President decided to relieve him of his command.

"So, it was your information that led to her taking that action," the younger advocate asked?

Joe looked at her and said that the information had resulted in the examination of the Colonel's behavior the actions she took was strictly up to her.

The older JAG thanked Joe for his time and hoped that the work on the project that he was leading went well.

Joe left the meeting, placed a call to Jorge and let him know that he felt that the JAG's were trying to somehow make that assassination attempt into some sort of conspiracy that the team might be involved in. He felt that perhaps they should get a chance to talk with the President and get some coaching from her.

Jorge chuckled and said that he and Jerry would help the two out and get them on track.

Joe then called Lydia and let her know that he had probably earned her an interview with the two the JAG's by the way he had answered some of their questions.

Lydia laughed and asked whether he had thrown his wife under the bus.

Joe laughed and said no he would never do that but he had no control over the runaway herd of cattle that was coming her way.

13 Change in Plans

14

<u>Through the Hole</u>

Ryan stood in front of everyone as he highlighted the fact that getting the second four person space craft, getting three doors with the attached living quarters completed were the two competing bottlenecks in the current plan. He added that his current plan would extend the time to launch by a month if the two bottlenecks could be overcome otherwise it might go out another month.

Joe stood up and walked to the front of the group, thanked Ryan for the quick development of the bottleneck plan, then added that neither the second four person craft nor having three door units would cause a delay beyond the thirty days. He emphasized that they could execute their journey with one of each. He preferred that they had everything so they could open up three regions of distant space however he preferred to have one successful journey than to accept another delay.

He asked Darian what he thought.

Darian was surprised by being asked. He looked at Samantha and then replied that since he was going to be the pig on this journey he would like it to be sooner rather than later. That got the response that he had been seeking as everyone laughed at his analogy.

They all knew of his reaction to accepting going through the Door his first time; "If a three hundred pound pig came out a pig when it went through and still thought he was a pig than I will do it."

Joe then asked if anyone objected to setting the date for the journey through the hole thirty days out and go if they had one of each of the two bottleneck items. No one raised any objections.

Jorge had been listening and liked how Joe had taken the lead. He might not have accepted being thought of as an Admiral but since the assassination attempt Joe had become much more active in guiding the team. He no longer waited to see what he, Tom or Linda were proposing. Joe had assumed total leadership of the Hole project. Jorge saw this as a very good thing and he noted that everyone on the team seemed to like the fact that Joe had gone up one step in his already top rung of the leadership ladder.

Lydia too felt that Joe's behavior had become much more assertive and direct. She saw that he had taken on a fresh, hands on, approach to all the activities on the project. She had asked him what had changed and was surprised when he replied that it was when he saw the red laser dot on her chest. He hugged her and said that his immediate reaction was to knock her over to get her out of harm's way even as he launched himself toward the President. He said it was then he realized that he needed to keep ahead of the bad guys. He added that when they had been kidnapped during the development of the Door he had taken the first step up but that situation did not threaten immediate death to any of them.

The attempted assassination had her, the president and himself in the cross hairs. It triggered a saying his father had taught him; "when you point a gun at a person, don't talk, shoot. Talk comes after the shooting." He added that it was time to quit talking about going through the Hole and take their shot. His one concern was that they be ready for whatever might happen when they went through. He wanted to make sure that everyone was willingly going through and that he had done everything ahead of time to keep them safe. The thought that had crossed her mind as she gave Joe and hug was, "the Admiral wants to ensure his fleet loses no ships."

Jorge spoke up and said that he was setting the launch date exactly one month out. He suggested that during the final week that all team members take time off and go home or to wherever they desired before they went off to some distant galaxy.

Samantha nodded and said he had a great suggestion and that she and Darian would be going to spend the week at her parents.

Joe said that he too would be spending the week with his parents and anyone wanting to ride the range would be welcome to come and enjoy being told stories and be fed by the greatest Uncle he had ever known.

H^3 said that he would take Joe up on his invitation.

Yara nodded and added that she and H^3 were going first to Brazil to her parents but would spend a few days at the ranch on their return.

Right after that Jorge asked if Joe's dad might be willing to host the whole team for two days.

Joe smiled and said that he would see. He figured his father and Uncle Ted would enjoy hosting the team for a couple of days but he figured he would let them decide and then make the invite and the arrangements.

The team left the meeting and Joe said that he wanted to go to the Odyssey for another walk through inspection.

Lydia commented that the team had done it several times.

Joe nodded and said that he still wanted to do it again and this time he wanted to do it differently. He said that he was going to use a stick, a rock, some tape and a contrary attitude and do everything that shouldn't be done.

General Delaney had overheard the discussion and asked if he could accompany him. He added that the first four seat space craft had been sent up to the Odyssey and they could do a contrarian check on it as well.

When Linda heard what Joe was planning she and Tom went through the Door up to the Odyssey and waited for him.

Lydia went up ahead of Joe and was surprised to be greeted by Linda who was holding a robe for her.

Joe was just as surprised to get the same treatment from Tom.

After all of them were in the control room Tom asked how Joe was going to get his stick, rock and tape up to the Odessey.

Joe smiled and said that he had recruited Aaron to send up a freshly cut maple branch cut from the tree that the Colonel had sat in during his attempted assassination.

He called down to Aaron and told him to send the branch through. He then held up the branch that had three smaller branches at the end and said that it was going to be the maple tree equivalent of a Roman Flagrum. He was going to added a small length of chain at the end of each of the small branches and then he was going to whip the equipment into shape.

Lydia laughed and said that she was going to hide all the ancient history books he had been reading because she didn't want him to come up with too many weird inspirations.

Joe led the way to the space suit dressing room and proceeded to get into his suit.

Tom and Linda both said that they would watch via the video system.

Lydia had donned her suit and was ready to accompany Joe.

General Delaney said that he would join the two when it was time to inspect the four person space craft but until then he would stay with Linda and Tom and watch Joe whip the equipment into shape.

Joe was enjoying the fact that he had surprised everyone with what he was planning. He did not expect any surprises but figured that doing something beat just sitting around waiting.

He led the way to the Hole generator cannon and began at the barrel end and worked his way back to the fuel source.

Lydia asked what he was listening for.

Joe shook his head and said that he was not sure and didn't expect to find anything but he felt the need to do something different. He laughed and said it was like the time they took a thirty foot RV from the truck lot and then tried to outrun a fast Camaro. It had been crazy then and what he was doing was crazy now. He laughed and said it was beginning to be a pattern.

He had worked his way along the barrel on both sides and had done the same with the lead fuel chamber. He then hit the first of the three power cable conduits that went to the fuel chambers. The sounds were dull thuds. The second cable sounded the same. Then when he flogged that third cable conduit there was a definite difference in the sound. It surprised him and he played his Flagrum across the three cable conduits.

Tom and Linda had a better audio feed than either Joe or Lydia.

Linda was amazed that the one cable conduit sounded hollow.

She spoke into the mike and told Joe that they would need to get that cable conduit checked out.

Joe raised his thumb to indicate that he agreed.

He then said he was moving on to inspect the auto lead fuel loading equipment. Nothing turned up there.

Tom meanwhile called down to Ryan and asked him to arrange to have a team sent up to check out cable number one to see if there was anything wrong with it.

Once the fuel loading equipment was checked Joe let General Delaney know that the four person space craft was next.

Everything seemed to be going well in checking out the craft until Joe tested the laser by not only using his Flagrum but by repeatedly firing the laser at the rock that he threw out in front of it.

They could see the red laser light hit the rock but there was no power in the red beam. The laser was dead and the light was a fake to simulate the laser.

The General found it hard to believe that anyone in his command had sabotaged the spacecraft. He said that he was personally going to figure out how it could have happened.

Joe came back into the suit room, took off his space suit and said that he was going back down, call a meeting together to discuss what he had discovered. He wanted to enroll Doug Hasterly the base security officer that he had gained great respect for during the hunt for the person who had leaked the information about the Door development. He looked over to the General and suggested that he too engage Doug to ensure that he had an unbiased person looking for the person or persons who were trying to sabotage the Hole effort.

The General said that he was going to take Joe's suggestion and meet with Doug as soon as he could after they all transited back to Earth.

Jorge was shocked when he learned what Joe had discovered. He wondered who had been able to infiltrated the security for the Hole project. He once again felt that the effort he was leading was in an espionage shadow war. He put in a call to President McAdam to set up a face to face meeting about a serious security issue.

14 Through the Hole

He was called back less than an hour later letting him know to come and meet with her as soon as he was able to get to Washington.

15

<u>Search for Sabotage Evidence</u>

Doug was not so much surprised by General Martinez's call than the fact that he was requested to come to a special meeting about security. He was sure that he had the best security team that anyone could possibly have.

The assassination attempt had greatly surprised him and he had called his team in and had given them a heated lecture about their failure. His team had, however, ultimately tracked down how the Colonel had been able to get on the base undetected and it had nothing to do directly with their security process. He concluded that the Colonel had arranged the resources that were available to him while he was the commander of the Piñon Canyon Facility. The failure was in giving the army the courtesy of letting them land directly on the Lakland base with out a check of the personnel entering. So, he counted it a as security flaw.

His one remaining disappointment was that his team had been a dozen of steps behind Joe when the shooting at the renaming ceremony had started.

When he walked into the meeting he went over to Joe and complemented him on his bravery and his promotion to the position of Admiral. He smiled and commented that it was the fastest anyone had ever gone from a seaman to Admiral. He was pleased to see that Joe took that in a good way as the two gave each other a hug.

Jorge looked around the room and called the meeting to order. He asked Joe to brief all of them about what he had found out.

Joe looked around the room and said that he had gone up to the Cosmos Odyssey to check things out in a backward, upside-down way to look for system weaknesses that would not be found under normal checkouts. He pointed out that the Hole cannon that had been mounted had not been fired and it was not planned to happen until the actual Hole generation was to happen. He had come up with an off the wall approach while he was reading a historic account of the Pharaoh's and later the Roman's use of the Flagrum to cruelly beat their slaves. He decided that he was going to beat on the equipment and he figuratively planned to do the same thing with all computer control systems.

Doug asked if he had any suggestions on how to find the saboteurs.

Joe nodded and suggested publicly highlighting how critical the three Door units would be to the success of the Hole project and make sure it got leaked both on Lakland and at the Marine Technical center. Then they should put each of the Door units and the living quarters that would be attached to the Door modules under surveillance to see if they could capture the people that were the floor operatives.

He added that he did not think the floor operatives would be the ones in command but gofers that were doing it for the money. They also needed a way to see who gave the orders to the gofers.

Doug suggested that he have his team check everyone working on the Door units and the living quarters and dig into all of their past communications and any other information they could find about them.

Joe volunteered that he and the rest of the team would be pleased to help in the internet search area if Doug thought that would be of help.

Doug smiled and said that he was sure that Joe's team members would be of significant help and he hoped they would be as successful as they had been in their previous internet search in finding the bad guys.

Linda asked what Joe had in mind in checking the computer programs.

Joe shook his head and admitted that he was not as comfortable in how to handle that process but he wanted to have her, Tom and H^3 take him backwards through their Hole generation program. He also wanted to go backwards through all the other programs. He thought that doing it on a white board would help highlight any defects. He wanted each part of every equation or line in the programs to be written out in English. He then stopped for a moment and said that before that he wanted every physical component examined for any defects.

Tom laughed and then let out a groan as he bent forward and put his head on the meeting table. He said that they would be working twenty hours a day and it still would take close to a year before they would be able to launch. He then let out another groan and said, "why did she make him an Admiral?"

Joe nodded and said that he would only agree to the launch date if the checks he was asking for were done.

He added that he was going to ask Lydia to be the leader of the physical inspection of every circuit board, interconnecting wiring, and power connection. He would see if Yara and Samantha would help to do those inspections.

He paused for a moment, looked at Doug and said that the only person left to help him was Darian and if he was paired with a good computer jock, Darian would take the search down the internet's rabbit hole.

Jerry spoke up and said that Doug could have his entire security team to work with. That would ensure that the hunt had a single leader. He wanted to discover who the people behind the sabotage happened to be and how they had been able to get to the hardware.

When Joe left the meeting he found Lydia and the rest of the team were sitting along the Hallway. He suggested that they all go for lunch and he would get them caught up on what was happening. On the way he added that he had offered Darian as their sacrificial lamb and Doug had accepted him. So, after lunch Darian should get in contact with Doug and find out what his fate would be.

He looked around and commented that the rest of them should not feel relieved because all of them were looking at twelve-hour days with their noses on the grind stone.

During lunch he let each of them know that he had insisted on a complete physical, electrical, electronic and programing detailed shake down and had volunteered each of them to a specific task.

He looked at Lydia and asked her to lead the physical inspection of all electronic circuit boards, the plugin frames, the electrical connections and power supplies and the environment where everything was mounted. He then asked Yara and Samantha to work with Lydia on an unbelievably large task. He added that he wanted the three to start with what was up on the Cosmos and toward the end schedule some night sessions to inspect the Doors and the associated lodging units. They should also inspect the second four person craft at night before it was sent up to the Odessey.

Yara nodded and asked when she should plan to sleep.

Joe looked at her and said that H^3 would not be getting much sleep either because he, Linda, Tom and H^3 would be going through all the programing that controlled the Cosmos Odessey.

He suggested that they all spend the afternoon getting organized and then early the next morning they would begin their meticulous, under the microscope inspection of everything.

That evening he and Lydia were sitting in their favorite seats in their upstairs living area. Lydia asked what had made him think about doing a last minute inspection.

Joe shook his head and said that it had come to him while he was reading about the treacherous politics during the Roman times. The thought of some global organization sabotaging the Hole effort came to mind.

I thought about the troubles we overcame getting the Door project to be a success and I realized that so far we had not faced any of the same obstacles on the Hole project. It struct me as an anomaly. I wondered if we had missed something or been distracted by the attempted assassination.

Lydia got up and walked over and sat on Joe's lap. She gave him a kiss and said that once again he was like the army calvary riding in to save the settlers from the attacking enemy. She said that she was glad to be on his side because the enemy always seemed to underestimate him.

Joe gave Lydia a responding kiss and said that he just wanted to make sure the two of them had a chance to take a couple more skinny dips in their favorite pond. He then smiled and said it was time for them to get bed.

The next morning after breakfast Joe said he would be meeting Linda and Tom at the earth side control center and H^3 would be the first one to be up on the Cosmos going line by line through the Hole control program.

Lydia said that she was meeting with Yara and Samantha and they would begin the physical inspection of every control system on the Cosmos. They planned to stay up there for the rest of the week to make it easier for them to put in the long hours they figured it would take.

Joe nodded and said that he would miss her but figured that he would be spending most of the time Earth side at the Hole monitoring control room.

As Joe was walking toward the monitoring control room he ran into Linda and Tom going there. After a quick greeting they all walked together. Once they got there, Joe checked to make sure the coffee pot had hot coffee. He took a cup and asked where he should sit.

Tom pointed to the table that he said they would use as they worked their way backwards, as Joe had suggested, through the lines of programs. He said that it would be impractical to write each line of code down but if there was a line of questionable code, they would capture that line, print it out, and put it on the white board that was against the wall of the room.

Linda asked why Joe wanted to go backwards through the program.

Joe smiled and said that he wanted H^3, her and Tom to think how things looked in the rear view mirror when they were driving their car and how it made their minds work differently than when looking through the front windshield. He felt that that difference would help if someone had changed or added any code.

Joe had refilled his coffee cup three times when the first line of questionable code came up.

It was Linda that called out the questionable code.

She ask H^3 why he had added a line of code to change a plus sign in the equation to a negative sign after a first time through.

H^3 replied that he was not the one that had added that line of code.

Tom spoke up and said that he had not added any lines of code to the programing so it appeared they had found a line of sabotage code. He wondered who would have enough expertise to do such a thing.

H^3 replied that adding the line of code to make such a change was an easy add for any programmer. No special high skill was required. The way the code was set up, it would change the sign once the Hole creation cannon fired. This meant that the change would only be noticed when the Cosmos Odessey was ready to return through the Hole and was ready to transit back. That would be like having someone pull the lead out of the distributor of a parked car. The driver of the car would only notice it when they returned to the car and wanted to leave the parking lot. He said that it was an ingenious way to sabotage the program without knowing how it was programed.

Joe suggested that they break for lunch and that afterwards they would continue checking the code. He said that he was placing a bet that they would find a similar line in the code for all major systems. He called Doug and ask him to identify anyone working on the Hole program with enough computing skill to add the line of code.

16

<u>Treasure Found</u>

Doug listened to what Joe was asking him to do. He said that he seemed to be experiencing DeJa'Vu and that Mathew Pinkerton III was once again at work through his various helpers.

Joe replied that he didn't think it was Mathew but it probably was connected to the network that Mathew had cultivated. Joe then said that he figured it would either be the Russian friends or maybe the Chinese connection that Mathew had. He went on and said that Doug should be looking for workers that had a Russian heritage and might have family connections that were being exploited.

After talking with Doug, Joe called Darian and informed him about that change in code that had been found and that he was looking for a person who was working on the Hole project as some sort of support that had good enough program skills to be able to enter a line of code into the Hole generator control program.

Darian asked if he was going to get any more details for his search.

Joe suggested that Darian might find someone with a Russian family background but that was speculation on his part.

Joe walked over to where Linda and Tom were sitting and saw that they had each selected a pastrami sandwich. He walked over and after a quick look decided that a BLT was what he wanted. He returned to the table with the sandwich and an iced tea.

He let them know that he had triggered the hunt for a person who was capable of inserting a line of code into the control program. He speculated that they would not find any more such lines in the control program for the Hole generator but he then said that he was betting on finding that line of code in every control program. He asked if there was a way that they could spend the afternoon doing a quick search for that line of code in every control program but not do it going line by line.

Tom replied that he thought that if he, Linda and H^3 spent a few minutes discussing how to do it they could set up a search routine and check the lines of code for all control programs.

After lunch, the three of them walked back to the meeting room where they reconnected with H^3 and got him updated.

H^3 said it would only take him a few minutes to generate the search code.

Tom meanwhile listed all the systems and their control programs. He had never thought about all the control programs and was surprised to find that the list was more than twenty.

Linda suggested they begin with the most critical ones such as the environmental system controls which had the air supply control system, the lighting control system, the heat control system, the waste handling system, the waste control system.

She then shook her head and said that she was not sure how many other systems fit under environmental.

H^3 had the search routine done and said that he would copy and paste the routine into every system they wanted to search.

Joe said that he was popping the cap off of a lemonade soft drink and if by the time he was done H^3 had installed the routine in all the systems that Tom and Linda had listed he would treat them all to as many rounds of beer or wine that they wanted.

H^3 laughed and said he figured he had all the time in the world because his routine would insert itself automatically into all the listed programs and as soon as he gave the routine the list he was going to transport down and meet all of them at the Officer's Club and let the Admiral start buying him drinks.

Joe lifted his soft drink and said that he would meet him there.

Tom looked at Linda and said that he wanted to sit at the end of the bar with the beautiful lady that had won him over the first time he had seen her and he too was going to let the Admiral buy them drinks.

Joe shook his head and said that he wanted to check with Lydia to see what they might have found.

Lydia, Yara and Samantha had almost immediately spotted a small square block mounted on almost every computer. They had immediately realized that the control systems were in miniaturized computer systems that were distributed around the Cosmos Odessey structure, but that the entire collection of physical elements would fit on a short two foot book shelf.

16 Treasure Found

What they discovered almost immediately was a small square one by one inch box about a quarter inch thick glued to the center of each of the flat cases that contained the systems. They had documented each find by taking a picture of the device but left all of them untouched. They had contacted Aaron and asked him to handle the investigation into the glued on boxes.

Aaron had been surprised to be called by Lydia. He agreed to investigate the objects that they had found. He reacted to Lydia's comment that she thought the objects were likely small explosives. He subsequently contacted Tobias, a bomb expert. He and Tobias transported up to the Cosmos.

After Lydia showed the two of them the object. Tobias asked them to stand back and in full protective gear he took an explosion proof container and removed one of the devices. They all let out a sigh of relief that nothing had happened. They went around and removed all the blocks that they had found.

About the time they were ready to transport back to Earth they got a call from Joe inviting them to the Officer's Club.

Lydia replied that they would be meeting him there as soon as they examined the treasure she and her team had found.

Once back on the ground, Tobias took them to the bomb blast area where he placed the devices in a larger bomb proof container. He then asked Aaron if he had any ideas how the devices might be activated.

Aaron took out his phone and showed Tobias and the rest an apt that he had written designed to make a program step through its lines of code. Since the bomb had been placed on a computer, he wondered if his Ap would be enough to trigger the bomb.

Aaron tried the Ap as they all stood behind the blast wall where Tobias had them standing. He shook his head when nothing happened.

He asked if it was safe to step out from behind the wall. After stepping to the side of the wall, he again tried the apt. Nothing happened. He looked around and shrugged his shoulders.

Before he could say anything, Samantha grabbed the phone from his hands and took twenty paces toward the bomb proof container and activated the Ap. She fell back laughing when the devices exploded. The blast had been contained but the noise had caused her to step back expecting to get hurt and in doing so she had ended up on her butt.

Tobias and the rest of them rushed to her to make sure she was alright. He helped Samantha stand and then chided her for taking such a risk. Lydia smiled and accused her of being influenced by her other half. She then suggested that they all go to the Officer's club and claim their reward.

Joe watched as Lydia, Yara and Samantha came in. He noted that Aaron was talking to someone that he did not know. It was clear to him that Samatha was the center of attention. He guided them to where the team had taken over a back area of the club.

He then said that they should give their orders to the two waitresses that were waiting on them. He walked over and introduced himself to the person who he had not met before.

Aaron announced that he had recruited Tobias, as a new member to the team who would be working around the clock to make sure they went on a safe trip.

Tobias, accepted a glass of beer from the waitress, smiled and said that his specialty was as a bomb disposal engineer. He pointed to Lydia, Yara and Samantha and thanked them for giving him the opportunity to be part of the team.

He pointed to Aaron and said that he was not only the person who had directly recruited him but who had given him a new tool to activate bombs. Then he walked up to Samantha and gave her a hug and said that she had almost made him have a heart attack when she detonated the bomblets that they had brought down. He then drank almost half a glass of beer and sat down.

Joe looked at Lydia and asked if Samatha's survival was her surprise or was the treasure she had talked about were the bomblets.

Lydia shook her head and said that it was not just one bomb but many bombs. She then pulled up the pictures she had on her phone and passed it around. She said the three of them had found them on almost all the main mother boards in the various computer systems. She smiled and said that Tobias and several helpers would be removing the devices and bringing them down to the bomb disposal area for the next month.

Darian had arrived in time to hear what Tobias and Lydia had to say. He walked over to Samantha and asked why she had taken such a risk.

Samantha shook her head and said that she had not taken any risk. Tobias had assured them that the bomb containment vessel was strong enough to handle an explosive at least fifty times larger than the small bomb that he had placed in the container.

Tom asked how many bombs or bomblets they had found.

Lydia retrieved her phone and looked at the list that she had compiled and said that they had found thirty seven bomblets but it was only the first day of looking.

Darian shook his head and asked who possibly had access to and the means to put that many bomblets into place.

Linda conjectured that it had to be someone who had been on the reconfiguration team of Doorship One into the Cosmos Odyssey.

Darian shook his head and said that Joe, Tom, H^3 and Linda had found some hacked code and had sent him looking for a hacker that could write the code to insert in the hole control program and they had not yet started looking at the myriad of other control programs and now Lydia and her team had found that a saboteur that had access to the ship had planted several dozen bombs. He then added that a historic security breach had occurred and he needed to contact Doug and see if they could figure out how to find how that could possibly happen on the most important top secret national project. He looked at Joe and asked if he had any additional guidance before he made a call to Doug.

Joe nodded and said that at least two individuals, that knew each other well and were working together were most likely involved. Every person that had been part of the transformation work needed to be investigated and persons that were close should especially be scrutinized. They had passed their top security investigations so they were more than likely sleeper agents that had worked together previously and had maintained their clearances over many years.

It would not surprise him to find a husband wife team, or brother-sister team.

Darian finished his first glass of beer and put in a call to Doug. He spent at least twenty minutes sharing what he knew with him. He then returned to the team and said that he had been told that Doug's team would work twenty-four seven following leads. He had been told to enjoy the reward celebration and in the morning be prepared to review what had been found.

Joe looked around and suggested that they hold off on any more celebrating until they had a ship that they were willing to risk their lives in. He added that he was going home and spend some quality time figuring out how he wanted to proceed. He looked at Linda, Tom and H^3 and said they should continue going through the many control programs. He let everyone know that he was going to ask for a meeting with Jorge, Jerry, and Doug to determine what they needed to do to ensure that as the sabotage work being removed it was not being replaced in some new way. They needed to get to the source of where the threat was coming from.

On the walk home he thanked Lydia for finding the physical bombs. He commented that they were exposing a very thorough sabotage effort. He looked at her and said that they had so far found that the programing and the equipment had been sabotaged. He asked her to refocus her team's effort and look for how the people on the team could be sabotaged.

Lydia frowned and wondered if any of the suits, seats, or the space where each person sat might be compromised. There was no food yet on the Odyssey other than snacks but she would make sure that anything that was to be taken up would now be scrutinized.

Joe nodded and said that he was going to insist on a very intensive search and inspection effort.

16 Treasure Found

17

<u>**A Hand from the Past**</u>

Mathew Pinkerton III sat in his small, spartan, windowless, sound proofed isolation cell. He had been in the cell for the last four years. He was under constant surveillance and had his food delivered through the port in his cell door. There was no chair. He sat on a poured concrete seat that came out of the wall. He had almost no contact with other inmates, staff and only an occasional visit from his great nephew.

He had been stripped of most of his wealth but the nephew to whom he had given his priceless art collection had located him and periodically visited. Mathew looked down at the nephew and thought him as not too bright but he came to enjoy his periodic visits.

Through him he had learned about another secret project the President seemed to be sponsoring. He so wanted to screw her over. He spent a great deal of time trying to figure out how he could reach out to the network he had built in his previous life as a cabinet member for the President. He figured the focus on revenge was one of the few things keeping him sane.

17 A Hand from the Past

Using his nephew and specifically worded job advertisements he was able to activate the communication protocol that he had previously set up. He reached out to his main contact and activated the sleeper network that he had put in place. He had put the network in place to help him when he was a free man but now he was unleashing it to get revenge on the bitch that called herself President of the United States. This was a person he hated with the utmost intensity and one that he was now determined to screw over.

The days in solitary confinement were spent with a focus on how to use the network he was activating and how to communicate his desires to the person now leading that network. He was sure that person was none other than a Russian, Dmitry Ivanov, a friend that he had made during his time in the President's cabinet. At that time, he had let Dmitry know who his sleeper activists were, how to activate them and guide them into the right position to carry out the sabotage that he hope would literally blow up in the Presidents face. He figured that he might be lucky take out a good number of the key people that supported her.

He was sure that his periodic cackling like laugh caused the guards monitoring his camera to think that he had gone over the edge. He wasn't too sure that he hadn't. The only thing that he knew was that he would finally extract an ounce of satisfaction in having taken down the person he considered his arch enemy. He would not only cackle he would shout his joy to high heaven if he was able to wreck the Presidents life.

Aliens We

Dmitry was methodically reading the want ads that he used to keep track of all his circuitous communications that he had with various political operatives. In the New York newspaper he used for such communications he recognized an ad placed by his acquaintance Mathew Pinkerton who he knew was now in a maximum security prison. He was a person that he did not like very much but who had shared with him a network that would be of great service to the motherland. He had reported his connection to the leadership and had received praise for establishing the connection and had been advised to stay in contact with the naïve American political.

When Pinkerton had been sent to prison Dmitry figured that the network had evaporated as well but he had stayed alert and was surprised when the messages from Mathew gave him access to the sleeper network. He was surprised to learn that the sleeper agent to activate that network was a person in the FBI. He was able to contact him by sending a courier with a disposable phone.

One morning as Lyle was getting a cup of coffee at the small coffee shop he stopped by every morning, a stranger handed him a phone, a card with a phone number who left without saying a word. The phone rang and a person identifying himself as Dmitry Ivanov a friend of Mathew Pinkerton III told him that he wanted to meet with him. Lyle said nothing and hung up. He did what the person who had recruited him had instructed him to do.

He returned to his office and arranged to take a vacation. He traveled to Gološeva, Latvia. He had never heard of the place but he learned that it was right on the Latvia – Russian border. Once there he used the burner phone to call Dmitry who agreed to meet him there and discuss what he was to do.

The very enjoyable dinner meeting that featured lamb chop, Pelmeni and grey peas also gave him the details that Dmitry said were being requested by his acquaintance, Mathew Pinkerton III. Lyle was very surprised that Mathew had been able to get a message out from his maximum security prison where he was not supposed to be able to communicate with the outside world.

The request however pleased him since he also despised the fact that a woman was running the country and that this would give him a chance to do something besides being bored carrying out his boring desk job. He had no idea what the top secret project that he was supposed help wreck was about but he figured he could wrangle getting the two sleeper saboteurs that he was to activate put on the project.

He and Dmitry hit it off and spent a very enjoyable evening drinking Iļģuciema kvass that tasted very much like a liquid malt loaf of bread. Dmitry gave him a phone that was to be used sparingly to communicate. He added the phone would not be traced to Lyle since it was registered under a fictious person in Russia.

After the meeting Lyle drove to Riga where he had hotel reservation in the pedestrian only Old Town.

The next morning after breakfast, he enjoyed himself by doing a little shopping, having a great lunch and dinner at two different restaurants and then spending an evening enjoying himself at a comfortable night club where he drank Riga Black Balsam and chased the shots with its unique, robust taste that hinted of bitterness, sweetness, and herbal flavor with large gulps of Valmiermuiža beer that tasted to him like flowery buckwheat honey. By the time he staggered back to his hotel he had spent a ton of money buying rounds for everyone sitting at the bar but he felt great about the evening.

The next day he flew back to DC and began the activation of the two names that Dmitry had given him.

Amber and Amanda were identical twins that had earned their electrical engineering degrees at Georgia Tech. They had been hired by a small local engineering company, Flawless Engineering LLC, run by Tobias Mistely. They got along great with their boss. They agreed with his political views and enjoyed having him take them on several boating outings on his yacht that he sailed out of Fort Lauderdale.

After talking with his friend Lyle , he worked to get Amber and Amanda top secret clearances so they could go to work on a top secret government project being done by one of the top aerospace companies. All he knew that they would be involved in the development of control system electronics.

Amber and Amanda went to work on the top secrete project but never learned what the project was about but they were commended for their great work. Then one day their boss let them know that he was terminating them but that he was recommending them to go to work for another firm that was working on another top secret project.

At first they were upset about their boss's actions but a few days later they learned that their salaries had gone up by almost fifty percent and realized that it was a way for their previous boss to indirectly reward them. They then were enthusiastic about the new work that they were undertaking.

They were quickly absorbed into the work their new company was involved in and found themselves much more in the know about a new project that involved a space ship that was being outfitted with a set of electronics and equipment that would revolutionize the ability to travel through space. It was then that they were contacted by Lyle Spencer from the FBI.

Amber immediately fell for him. He let them know that he had a special request. They were to place small special explosives on the electronic control boards and various other locations on a spaceship that was being modified for a special mission. He admitted that he was not aware of what the special mission was but they were likely to find out when they went to work on doing the startup of the spaceship that was being refitted for that mission. They would get trained to operate out in space and be doing the startup and check out of all the control systems.

Aliens We

The two of them admitted to each other that they felt a little guilty rigging the spaceship for failure but they were very happy with the money that showed up in their new Jamaican offshore bank accounts. The work that was going on took them into a world where they felt they had entered an alternate universe.

As they carried out their subversive actions they began to feel more and more guilty but they agreed that the guilt was overshadowed by their new found wealth and their trips to the Bahamas and Hawaii. It was only when they were asked to put their bomblets into the spaces that would directly injure and maim the team that would fly the spaceship that they felt guilty enough to question what they were doing but by then they agreed that they were in too deep to stop. They figured a few days relaxing on the beach would help them get rid of their feelings of guilt.

They finished the horrible work that they had been paid to do and decided that they would quit their current employment and spend a few months enjoying the Bahamas. They quit, left their apartment, and went to the Bahamas.

Darian almost missed the names of the two people that had been part of the startup team because of the fact that they had quit the company that had done the startup. They were no longer listed as employees of the company that had provided the people with top secret clearances for the startup of the conversion electronics on the Cosmos Odessey.

He realized that he had actually seen the two when they had transported up to the Cosmos and had laughed about his reaction to the two very good looking blonds. He had reminded himself that he already had the most beautiful woman that he was in love with but his eyes still seemed to pick out good looking women.

He checked to see if he could find their current address and learned that they had moved and had not left any forwarding address. He had their names and figured he would be able to find them by doing a data search. When that failed he knew that he had most likely found the person's responsible for the placement of the bombs.

He checked more deeply into their back grounds and found that both of them had electrical engineering degrees but they also had minors in computer programing. He shared his findings during the afternoon meeting of the security team.

Doug listened to what Darian had learned, thanked him, and said that his team would take over. He knew that Joe was ready to have his team come back together and focus on their upcoming mission. The bomb removal team had found what they were sure were all of the bombs. They commented that whoever had planted all the bombs was ruthless in their thoroughness and had shown no mercy when it came to how they would have injured and mutilated that crew.

Darian was relieved to turn over the search and the capture of the two saboteurs to Doug's team. He was ready to focus on the upcoming trip through the Hole. He hoped it would be a trip that was now safe.

As Doug took over the search for the where abouts of the two saboteurs, Amber and Amanda were relaxing and enjoying the sun on the beach. After a few drinks and working on their tans, their guilty feeling seemed to go down like water on the beach at low tide. Little did they know that it would be the last few days of their lives that they would spend outside of a maximum security prison. Little did they know that they would be sharing similar cells in the same prison that Mathew Pinkerton III was in. Little did they know that the money that they had accumulated would also evaporate. And, and little did they know that they would serve thirty years in prison and would possibly have the chance to get out as old women who had missed most of what could have been very enjoyable lives.

Mathew Pinkerton II's hand had reached out from the past, had failed at extracting his revenge but had ruined their futures.

17 A Hand from the Past

18

<u>Moving On</u>

Jorge listened to what Doug was sharing at the morning meeting of the Hole team.

Doug credited Darian for having tracked down two sisters that had planted the bomblets throughout the Cosmos Odessey. He went on to say that the sisters were yet to be apprehended but he was sure it was only a matter of time before that occurred.

Jorge thanked Doug and Darian and then said that he was taking the information to share with the President and planned to ask her to take over the apprehension of the two on the floor operatives and the subsequent discovery of the people that he was sure went upward from the two. He stated that he wanted Doug to focus on very tight security around the Hole team in the remaining few days before their departure. He wanted Joe to get the team ready to go through to wherever the destination might be.

Joe said that he was ready but he wanted to know the source of that had initiated the sabotage. He had a suspicion that it was the same nemesis that had tried to sabotage the Door project and he was interested in verifying his suspicion.

18 Moving On

Jorge called an end to the morning meeting but asked Joe to stay for a few minutes.

Once everyone had left, Jorge asked Joe what he was thinking.

Joe shook his head and said that he felt that he would begin with Mathew Pinkerton III and see who his visitors were and then the determine how often they visited and what their actions were after each visit. He went on to say that he suspected someone in the US government establishment in the CIA or the FBI that was an associate of Mathew. He would want whoever was running the investigation to look for any links to some overseas country that Mathew had a close relationship or affinity to.

Jorge asked why Joe had the suspicion that he was voicing.

Joe shook his head and said that he had no idea why he was thinking what he was thinking other than so far it was that one individual that had been at the root of all their attacks. Yes there was the kidnapping of he, Lydia and Darian that probably had its roots in China but they had not tried to get into the project after that.

Jorge nodded and said he was going to set up a meeting with the President to turn over the apprehension of the two saboteurs and he would share what he had just been told.

Joe said that he should say hello to the President for him and that as always he was looking forward to their next meeting.

When he got to the team room, Tom was getting ready to describe what he hoped they would find on the other side of the Hole that they would go through.

Joe nodded and asked which of the three Holes he was talking about.

Linda spoke up and said that she and Tom had been discussing all of the three. They were working with Aaron in the development of a routine that would use the visual, the infrared, ultraviolet, x ray, gamma ray frequencies of light to detect any signs of life. They felt that it should be one of the major efforts of the team. She added that once they were on the other side of the Hole they should spend the first few days doing a search of the area as well as very accurately determining the exact position of the Hole they had created. Then if they found some planet that might show the signs of having life they could approach it and see if it was intelligent life that they could communicate with.

Yara asked who their language specialist happened to be.

Tom laughed and said that they had a Brazilian, a member with a Texan drawl, two true English speakers from the UK, a Vietnamese capable member and three American language speakers. He added that between them they had many of the variations of the worlds languages and should feel capable of communicating with a foreign sounding language.

Joe shook his head and asked if it was possible to send communications through the Hole.

Tom admitted he did not know but felt that the only way to do so currently would be to send a recorded communication back through the Hole via a rocket or send someone through the Door to the one on base.

Joe nodded and suggested that they should augment the Earth bound team with several linguistic specialists and they should verify their ability to send a recorded message back to Earth once they were through the Hole.

He asked if Samantha was willing to take on the role of handling the communication back to Earth.

Samantha nodded and said that it would be an honor to do so.

He asked if Yara would take on the role with Lydia to communicate with any intelligent beings that they might come in contact with.

Yara, looked at Lydia, saw her nod in the affirmative and replied that she too would be honored to do so.

He looked at Tom and Linda and asked that they be the ones to manage the search for intelligence once they were through the Hole.

H^3 asked what he should be doing.

Joe shook his head and suggested that he check all the control systems to make sure that everything had worked as he had intended.

He then pointed at Darian and said that, once through the Hole, he should inspect the external environment on the Cosmos to ensure that there was no damage.

He paused for a moment and said that he was going to reduce the stress that he was sure he would have once they arrived at the other side of the Hole and he would sit back and sip on a beer while they all worked their butts off. He got the laughter that he had been seeking.

He them said that he was going to insist that he be taken by the hand and shown all the physical areas that had been checked and that he again be taken through the programing code this time he would be the guide going through the code. He then said that the entire team would don their space suits and do a detailed check of the entire exterior of the Cosmos Odessey. He paused for a moment and asked who had done the inspection of the suits. The silence that settled on the room was all he needed. He said that before putting on the suits they should be closely examined and before they went out he wanted them to wear the suits inside the ship for at least two hours.

Lydia shook her head and commented that there did not seem to be an end to the potential areas for sabotage.

Linda said that she agreed and it was annoying but she was going to do as their Admiral insisted and she was going to make sure that every inch of everything was checked.

Yara spoke up and said that she had been the one that had worked with the space suit maker to make each individual suit so she would lead the checkout of the suits.

Joe said he would appreciate her doing so. He wanted to caution her to do a physical check before doing a suit activation. He said he was betting on suit activation being the trigger for any bomb and that the bomb location would be in the chest area of the suit.

After a few moments he said that he was going to ask for additional help for each of them. As much as he wanted to personally check every physical inch of the Cosmos Odessey he had just come to the realization that the task was a bigger log than they could cut on their own during the short time period they had before making their first trip through the Hole.

He walked down the hall to Jorge's office and asked to speak to him. He explained what he wanted to do and the fact that he needed at least thirty people to help with another round of searches for additional explosives. He let Jorge know that once the spaces suits were cleared by the bomb squad, he and the team would do an external inspection while the people he was requesting would do an inch by inch inspection of the internal part of the ship.

Yara worked with Tobias and his bomb squad to get the spacesuits thoroughly examined for any bombs that might have been planted. She had them feel every inch of the lining as she opened up the control console that went across the inside of the suit and checked there for any foreign object. After the first suit was cleared she took out the helmet that was a separate unit. Almost immediately she spotted an object in the top of the helmet buried in the lining.

Tobias said that he preferred to take the helmet back to the ground to remove the object.

Yara said that she had no objection but they should do a quick inspection of all the helmets since getting the helmets down to Earth would require a shuttle to come up to retrieve them.

Tobias looked around and asked if there was a space where the helmets could be isolated where the bomblets could be taken out. He would then have the bombs taken down to be disposed of.

It turned out that there were no bomblets in the suit but every helmet had one at what was the very top of the skull area.

Yara shook her head and said that a bomblet exploding in the helmet would essentially blow up the skull of the person wearing it. It was as horrifying of a sabotage as she could think of and she hoped that the persons who had done such a thing would spend the rest of their lives in prison.

She called Joe and let him know what she had found.

Joe thanked her and asked that she have the bomb squad search for similarly places that would maim the person sitting in their seats or operating their control system. He chuckled and suggested checking the restrooms as well.

Yara asked Tobias to have his team check the places Joe had suggested.

Tobias came back a short time later and said that the bomb hunt reminded him of his yearly search for morel mushrooms. His teams would go past a check, he would take another pass, and he would find a bomblet. He said that his team was learning more about how to find bomblets then any of them wanted to learn. He wondered how much time the persons planting the bomblets had spent doing it or how they had chosen where to plant them.

Yara shook her head when she was shown where the bomblets had been place. They would have blown off feet, hands or exploded under someones butt. The more she learned the more she knew that those placing the bombs were heartless.

Yara reported where the bomblets were being found.

Joe reacted immediately by calling Doug and asked him to pass the information on to whomever was going to arrest the two women who had planted the bomblets. He asked that they be charged with attempted murder for each bomblet that targeted one of his team members. He added that so far each of his team members would have faced more than six life taking bomblets. He said that would make forty-eight attempted murder charges that each should be charged with.

Doug chuckled and said that he too would like to make sure the two faced not only those forty-eight charges but given the number of bomblets the two should face the death penalty. He said that he would talk with Jorge to ensure that the President's team now handling the apprehension of the two and those who would then prosecuted the two would have all the details of what was being found on the Cosmos Odessey.

Jorge assured him that he would be pushing for the death penalty.

19

<u>Going Through</u>

A week later, Joe sat at the control station ready to press the button to fire the Hole generation cannon.

He started to move his hand to press the fire button and stopped. He quietly asked everyone to activate their control consoles and let him know when they had done so. He then said that they would all press the fire button at the same time on his count and then they would all fire the dust clearing rockets and finally they would sent the USS Cosmos Odessey through the hole. They would all participate at the same time on his count. He said the count would be, one, two, three, fire.

Lacey, her cabinet members, and the Chiefs of Staff were all sitting in the situation room of the White House watching and listening to the launch. She was as excited as the time Joe had saved the team of Doorship One. She commented that Joe, by getting all of his team to be part of the launch, had ensured that each of those team members would follow him into hell if he asked them to.

19 Going Through

The Chief of Staff responded and said that he would be one of those that would follow Joe anywhere as well. He said he had been shouting like crazy when Joe had accelerated the capsule that the Doorship team was on and then had his team figure out a way to reach the module had stopped short of the Doorship after the capsule had run out of fuel.

Joe quietly announced that Hole generation would occur on his count. He then counted; "one, two, three, fire."

He had he team then fire the dust clearance rockets when the Hole appeared. The firing went on for a few moments and when it did not seem to be slowing down, Joe ordered the Door and living unit to be sent through and moved to the side of the designated landing area.

He then asked Linda to send the designated mouse through the Door and see if it survived to return back.

A few moments later Linda announced that the mouse was back and still seemed to be a mouse.

Tom stood up and said that he was going to follow the mouse and would get all the information that he could about what was on the other side.

A few moments later, Tom called out that they must have chosen a dusty spot to try to make the entrance. He went on to say that he was recording everything and would be bringing the recordings back with him for study by the team waiting for it back on Earth.

Lacey looked over to her Science Advisor and said that she wanted him to participate with the analysis team located at the Lakland base. She wanted to know what they learned about that location of the Universe and whether she should sponsor a return to that region. She turned her attention back to the monitoring screen.

Tom put the recorded information in the capsule on one of the through the Hole rockets that was attached to the living quarters, adjusted its aim so that it would reach a point near the Cosmos Odessey and launched it.

The return of the rocket achieved several critical things. First it verified that once the Cosmos Odessey went through the hole it could return back to its original location. Second it verified that there was a way for information to be sent back even when the Cosmos did not chose to go through the hole. Finally, it provided the information that would let what Tom had done to be automated.

Joe had arranged that the automation was applied to any adjustments that Tom and H^3 decided was needed and it would be done immediately after Tom returned.

Once Tom returned and was at his seat, Joe asked H^3 to put the coordinates for their second try into the control system.

He asked Linda if the Hole generation cannon's fuel had been replenished.

Linda replied that the refueling had been completed.

He again reminded everyone that they were to participate in firing the Hole generation cannon.

He then counted; "one, two, three, fire."

19 Going Through

The second Hole appeared and six scout ships went through and began firing their lasers. Once again the firing went on for several minutes and it was not slowing down. Joe ordered the Door and living unit to be sent through.

Joe commented that there was no way of knowing if the automated system of data gathering was working. He would give the automated data gathering system fifteen minutes to do its work, then a five minute grace period before moving on. He suggested everyone relax, take a break and then be back in their seats in exactly twenty minutes. He got up and announced that he was going to take a walk around the ships walk way. He was followed by everyone but Tom and H^3.

H^3 looked over to Tom and said that he was getting everything ready for the third try. He added that Joe had asked him to get the remaining through the hole clearance lasers programed. He wanted every remaining laser deployed because he wanted to ensure the opportunity to go through.

Tom nodded and said that they had eighteen laser rockets left.

H3 nodded and began programing the coordinates that would position them in a sphere around the area where the Cosmos would be located when it came through.

Lacey had taken the opportunity during the break to have those in the room discuss what this technology meant to the world and how the US should manage the control of such a technology.

The Chiefs immediately commented that the US would not need rockets to protect the country because the Hole technology would allow it to respond to aggression with precise, focused destruction of the enemies weapons.

Her secretary of Defense spoke up and said that huge savings could be accomplished by having a smaller military and more precise ways of responding to threats.

Lacey nodded and said that they needed to focus on making all of this happen in the next couple of years so that her vice president would win the upcoming election. She pointed at the screen as Joe returned from his walk and sat down and said that she hoped Hole number three would work out.

The rocket that the Odessey had been awaiting from the second Hole came back through the Hole and was brought on board.

He then said that he would have to fire Tom and his astronomer team members if the third location was as dirty as the first two. He wondered why Tom and his team selected such dirty places.

Tom gave a chuckled, said that he had come prepared for this exact situation and that he knew which astronomer team member he would recommend to have fired.

Joe shook his head and suggested that Tom go and get into the third Door living unit and go through with it on the third and final hole and make sure he had enough food to last for a lifetime.

Tom made as if to get up and leave his seat.

Joe then asked everyone to say a prayer and get ready for the third hole.

He reminded the monitoring team on Earth that they would need to take control of any returning rockets that would be bring back information and bring the rockets down to the designated landing area.

Lacey looked over to her science advisor and asked if he was aware of this capability. When she saw him shake his head negatively, she asked him to contact General Martinez and ask that the President be put into the loop. She was surprised that the General had not informed her.

Joe then quietly commented that the third time had to be the charm. He then held up his hand and slowly recited the count down.

The Hole opened and the swarm of eighteen rockets with their dust clearing lasers swooped through the hole and went through an intense round of firing. Joe let out a whoop when suddenly they all shutdown.

He announced that it was the USS Cosmos Odessey's turn. He asked everyone to get ready and slowly began the count; "one, two, three, fire."

The Odessey was suddenly at the center of the giant sphere that had been cleared by the eighteen lasers.

Jorge, Jerry, and Doug let out a whoop as the Odessey disappeared from view. They were sitting with a group of Jerry's astronomer and science team members who had been rapidly assembled at Joe's request.

Joe had realized that if information could be sent back through the Hole by rocket, that information needed to be retrieved, and analyzed. That team had literally been brought together in the last day. They had worked with Tom and H^3 to select the hole coordinates but had not been asked to be the analysis team until a day ago.

The team was made up of four people that would most likely need to be augmented with additional capabilities that would need to be determined if information rockets actually came through the hole.

When the rocket returned from the second hole, Jerry had commented that they needed to get additional small rockets ready to go through the hole so they could pass information back to the Odessey.

Jorge agreed and asked him to get several dozen rockets ready. He then sent a message to the President to bring her up to speed.

Shortley after she was given the message, Lacey sent a reply thanking the General for getting her caught up on what now seemed to be a fast moving project. She informed him that the two saboteurs were in the process of being apprehended and that she had instructed the team doing the apprehension to make sure not to accidently kill them. She wanted them to face trial and if found guilty face the maximum sentence that could be imposed by law. She was aware that she was extremely biased and wanted the two of them to suffer but more than that she wanted to find out who had been their handlers and get them as well.

19 Going Through

When Jorge received the President's reply, he decided to share the fact that Joe felt that Mathew Pinkerton III was somehow behind the sabotage that Joe felt that the sabotage was being carried out by a sleeper group that he had somehow been able to activate.

Upon receiving the General's reply, Lacey instructed her team to take a close look at Mathew Pinkerton's connection to the outside world from his maximum security cell. She took Joe's suspicion seriously and instructed that if he had any visitor, that visitor's every action was to be investigated in great detail.

Jorge returned to the monitoring and ask if there had been any information returning through the Hole. He was disappointed that nothing had been sent. He wondered how Joe and his team was doing on the other side of the Universe.

20

<u>On the Other Side</u>

Joe asked Lydia to make a quick sweep of the space around them and let him know the situation. He asked H^3 to rotate the lasers so they formed a defensive sphere. He asked Tom to transit to the Door and record all the information that he had done two times before and then send the information rocket back through the Hole.

Darian and Samantha were busy checking the operation of all the on board systems to make sure that they had all made the transit through the Hole without any damage.

Yara asked what he wanted her to do.

Joe smiled and said that she, Linda, and himself were going to go to the ships kitchen and put in a pot pie for everyone, fix a mixed salad and set the table for lunch.

Linda laughed and asked if pot pie was the best he could do.

Joe shook his head and said that they needed to work with whoever was the one that had chosen the food that was sent with them. Except for a couple of days of lettuce, a few tomatoes, and some onions everything else was frozen dinners.

Tom returned and said that they were at the edge of a solar system that had twelve planets circling a star slightly larger than the Sun.

"Well, the third time seems to have been the charm," Joe commented as he took a bite of his pot pie.

Everyone was enjoying having a hot meal even if it was only a pot pie when alarms started blaring. They all rushed to their designated stations. Their stationary stations were different than their transit stations.

Joe was at the same station. Darian was at the left laser control station. Yara was at the right laser control station. They each controlled twelve lasers. Lydia was at the communication control station. Tom and Linda were at two different observation stations ready to record whatever they aimed their instruments at. Samantha and H^3 were assigned as backups to Darian and Yara.

Joe asked what the alarms were about.

Tom responded that he had an incoming rocket moving at supersonic speed.

Linda said that she too had the incoming.

Yara spoke up and said that she had three lasers zeroed in on the missile that was about fifteen minutes out.

Joe asked if Lydia had any messages coming in.

Lydia replied that she did not.

Tom said that he had some signals that seemed to be exchanges with the incoming missile.

Joe nodded and said that the missile would most likely explode before it reached the target and spew out a huge number of smaller bombs that each would be dangerous.

He gave the order for Yara to take the missile out.

Yara fired each laser separately and hit the missile three times from the tip to the tail. The missile blew apart but its contents followed its final trajectory. This was a trajectory that had been altered by the first laser hit on the nose. The bundle of smaller bombs followed that trajectory.

Tom announced that none of the smaller bombs were going to come any closer than about two hundred miles.

Linda said that she had identified the planet that had launched the missile by back tracking the missile's path. It was the seventh planet from the star.

Samantha laughed and said that at least they had found life smart enough to make a sophisticated missile but she wondered how intelligent they were.

Darian said that they were certainly aggressive, and they must be scared that aliens had come to enslave them.

Lydia shook her head and said that she had always wondered if aliens existed, now the next time she looked in the mirror she would know that she was seeing one.

"We are the Aliens," she announced loudly.

And those on the planet are very afraid of us even though they seem to be well armed.

Linda replied that they seemed well armed but they did not have any satellites circling the planet so they must be early in their development of space travel.

Joe said that he would like to send a series of signals to the planet to see if they could learn more than about the beings that had launched the missile.

Let's send them a series of greetings that basically say we are friendly. Let's also get ready to make a mini Hole that allows us to send the small four person module through. If they don't try to shoot it out of an orbit around their planet we will go to it and see if we can set up a communication system that sends information back to Earth.

Lydia asked what the aliens should say to those scared people down on that planet.

Linda suggested sending down a picture of one of them with an open hand.

Joe asked if their sensors could pick up any information from some sort of communication that might be present on the planet.

They aimed all their different sensors at the planet trying to get information that might be of help.

Samantha said that there was a rich mix of different frequencies. She was trying to determine which were audio, which might be visual and in what frequencies they were occurring.

H^3 cubed said that he was running all the captured signals through several of his Aps trying to decipher them.

About an hour later he let out a whoop and said that he had a visual of what the beings on the planet looked like.

Everyone stopped what they were doing to look at the big screen that they had set up in their largest meeting room that was now being used like a command center.

Joe took a look and declared that they had found Frog world.

Tom noted that they were bipeds and had four fingers with an opposing digit much like his own hand.

Lydia added that there seemed to be two general sizes of the beings. She wondered whether like frogs the larger ones would be female.

Joe suggested they send a picture of two of them back to the planet to see if they could start a conversation with them.

It was only a few minutes after they had sent the pictures when they got a return picture of the a larger of the species holding two small versions of itself and the smaller of the two pointing at the larger being.

Joe said that it seemed that Lydia was right. He asked if anyone had a family picture that they could use to reply.

Linda said they had a picture of her daughter's family that had her breast feeding her youngest and her oldest daughter at her shoulder and her husband with his hand on the older daughter's shoulder. It was very similar to the picture that had been sent up to them.

Joe looked at it and said that it was a perfect response. He said that Lydia should send it as their response. He commented that they had been at it for more than fourteen hours and they needed to get some rest.

Tom suggested sending them an image of him during the day and an image of him in the dark of night. He commented that those on the planet should understand the message.

Joe suggested they follow up with a picture of the Cosmos in the daylight and the Cosmos in the dark. Then light up our hull and then turn off all exterior lights. This would let the people on the planet know that they lived in a day and night cycle like they did.

They got what they thought was a positive response and Joe suggested that they take two actions. He asked H^3 to prepare to move the Door into an orbit around the planet. He asked Tom to send the information they had gathered back through the Hole to Earth and request translation support for the messages they had so far exchanged with the planet and a request to have a translation team set up at Lakland. He added that the communication should include a request for a representative that could negotiate with the beings on the world that had been found and a special team that could establish meaningful, full communications with the beings on the planet. He added that those people were frightened by the appearance of the USS Cosmos Odessey and would need reassurances that Earth had no desire to take over their world.

He said that he was going to try to get some sleep and suggested that everyone wrap up what they were doing and get ready for some long days.

He reminded Tom that the folks that they needed could come one at a time via the Door and that they had plenty of space on the Odessey as well as supplies.

Aliens We

Jorge had been awakened when the message came in from the Cosmos Odessey He had been waiting to learn what the Odessey team might find but he had never anticipated such a find. He was floored but immediately copied the President.

The news hit Lacey like a sledge hammer hitting a post being driven into hard ground. She had never dreamt that life that had missile technology would be found on the very first mission. She knew immediately who the person to represent the US would be and the rest of the world and he was already there. She instructed that a team of linguists and a mix of specialists in a variety of fields be sent in support. She deferred to General Martinez on the number that would be sent to the Odessey.

Joe knew that the news would shake up everyone associated with the Hole project. He was trying to grasp the enormity of finding very intelligent life. He was also worried about establishing a friendly working relationship with the beings that looked very much like walking, bipedal frogs. He wondered what their diet might be and what if any help Earth could be to the planet that they had not yet discussed a name for. It was hard for him to get to sleep. Lydia had her hand on his chest and had wished him a good night and seemingly immediately fell asleep. He would have liked to discuss his thoughts with her but decided that a breakfast conversation with the rest of the team was the next best thing. He did not know when he fell asleep but when he awoke he was alone in bed.

He got up, got ready for the day, and then walked out to the cafeteria area. Everyone but H³ and Samantha who together had the last watch were there.

Darian gave him a hard time about sleeping in.

Joe looked at the clock and realized it was only six in the morning their time. He wondered what time it was for the people that they had been communicating with. As soon as he realized he was thinking of them as people he felt better.

Lydia brought him a single pancake with melting butter and an over easy egg on top. She put the bottle of maple syrup down next to the plate.

Joe thanked her and proceeded to smother the pancake with maple syrup. He looked at Tom and asked him if food could be transported up via the Door.

Tom said he thought so but he had never tried. He would send a message to have Jorge send up some eggs, a head of lettuce, a head of cabbage, bacon, and some ham.

Linda commented that she thought those items would come through if they were fresh enough. She added that it would be a real win if a food supply chain could be set up.

A missile from Earth came through the Hole. Everyone wondered what message they would find.

When he missile came through, Joe said that the Door might provide one path for food to come to them but the rocket through the Hole might provide a much better one.

He commented that perhaps the Door would be the avenue for the people skill they needed and a resource replenishment rocket would be a better route for food and other things to get to them.

20 On the Other Side

21

<u>Grog of Anura</u>

Grog was appraised of an alien spaceship that had mysteriously appeared and put on a display of fire power. He had counseled a wait and see approach but had been over ridden by the council who had issued orders for an immediate display of the power they had and perhaps end the invasion of the Aliens.

The rocket which they had prepared as a way to combat their mortal enemies on Wŭ loaded with mini explosives was on the launch pad ready to fire. They ordered its immediate launch to take out the Aliens.

He was disappointed that the council was so frightened of the appearance of the Alien vessel. It did not appear to be formattable to him. He had his team at the telescopes monitoring the vessel in all frequencies. He had another part of the team monitoring all communication frequencies. As he reviewed the initial Alien display of their power he noted that it had all been aimed inward from objects that made a huge sphere and he noted an object that appeared and moved to the edge of that sphere. It was a few moments later that the ship had appeared at the center of the sphere.

Then when the missile from the surface was half way to its target he noted that the objects that he now thought of as laser cannons turned outward and several homed in on the rocket and blew it up.

His team let him know that the launch location had been painted by frequencies from the Alien vessel. He anticipated an angry and violent response but no retaliatory action was taken. Instead, there were a series of signals from the Aliens. It was apparent to him that they were trying to communicate with those on his planet.

The council had ordered the firing of the only long range missile that was at their disposal. All other missiles were dramatically smaller and would not be able to reach the Aliens. They recognized their misjudgment and gave him full authority to communicate with the Aliens but he was ordered not to surrender any of their world to them.

He was surprised when his team received a picture of two of the Aliens. They had eyes that seemed to sit in their skull and were protected by eyelids very much like his own. However, it was clear to him that they were not water creatures because they had hair like lashes on the eyelids. They, unlike himself, had a breathing projectile that rose out between their eyes. He had two nostrils but they were flat on his face. They also had what appeared to be teeth in an opening below their nostrils that were set in a strong looking jaw. His jaw by comparison was almost nonexistent while theirs looked very strong and protruded below the mouth.

He then noted what he took as their arms and hands. They were very much like his own but their fingers did not have the suction pads at the end as the digits on his.

All in all, they did not appear as different as the various stories about Aliens had led him to believe.

As a response, he sent them a picture of himself, his mate and his two off spring.

In return he received a picture similar to his of a being with red hair pointing to a being that held two off spring.

Unlike his species, the red haired being was significantly larger than the being with the two off spring. From this he concluded that one difference was that the being that gave birth was the smaller of the species. The was opposite of his species.

He was also surprised that the Aliens had a wake sleep cycle similar to his own and was very pleased when he understood the display of light and dark on the exterior of Alien's ship. It had taken most of the light cycle to work through the communications with the Aliens and he was ready to sink into the warm water and let his mind float and get some sleep.

When he returned on the next wake cycle, he found his team in an agitated state because the vessel was now located much nearer the planet and was in the same orbital path as the planet and the strange object that had been on the edge of the laser blasting sphere was now in orbit around the planet.

He calmed them all down and suggested that they re-establish communication with the Aliens to see what more they could learn.

An image showing one of the Alien's sitting and eating was displayed on the screen. He did not know what was being consumed but he got the idea. He replied with a picture of himself snacking on some dried seaweed.

He was astounded when the Alien displayed a piece of sea weed that looked like the one he had been eating. He was even more astounded when a clear box with four strips of seaweed appeared on the floor of the communication room.

He looked at the box and its content and realized that the Alien powers were well beyond what existed on Anura. Perhaps he thought he should be afraid. He picked up the box and held it up for his female camera person to film him.

He then sent a grouping of the different members of the Anura dominant species. There were some six thousand different Anuran beings. He wondered how many versions there were of the aliens.

When only four differing pictures were returned he was once again stunned. There was a white, a brown, a tan, and more yellowish version of the beings. To have so few variations seemed to be incomprehensible. He wondered what else he would learn that was going to be totally strange to him.

Joe had been on the other end of the exchange.

He asked Samantha to generate his name in the top twenty languages in the world.

It only took her a few moments to generate a list of the top twenty.

He looked it over and suggested that they drop the languages that duplicated his name in the same scrip.

With Samantha's help he had a list of his name in twenty different languages. He then had her drop off any language that had the same translation of his name.

1. English: The world's most spoken language, with 1.5 billion speakers around the world; **Joe**.
2. Mandarin Chinese: with 1.11 billion speakers; 乔
3. Hindi: with 615 million speakers; जो
4. Spanish: with 560 million speakers; **José**
5. Arabic: with 422 million speakers; **ju**
6. Bengali: with 273 million speakers; জো
7. Portuguese: with 264 million speakers; **Zé**
8. Russian: with 255 million speakers; **Джо**
9. Urdu with 230 million speakers; جو
10. Japanese: with 125 million speakers; ジョー
11. Marathi: with 99 million speakers; जो
12. Telugu: with 96 million speakers; జో
13. Tamil: with 89.6 million speakers; ஜோ
14. Korean: with 81 million speakers; 조

He figured that fourteen versions of his name would be enough.

He then set up his message with his picture, the number 1 and Joe

Then he again set up his picture, the number 14 and Joe and all the remaining versions of Joe. He had the list simplified to only have the language and that version of Joe.

He then asked Samantha do the same with her picture and name and keep the same order for all the languages.

He then set up another message with his picture, 1 a picture of Earth and the number 8,000,000,000.

He then set up another message with the picture of the person that he understood to be named Grog, a picture of the planet that he understood was called Anura and left the remainder of the line blank.

The rest of the day was spent sending and receiving messages to clarify the initial set that had been sent.

He was aware that as he and Samantha were focused on sending and responding to a series of messages, there were people arriving from Earth. They were brought in, briefly introduced and given seats to the back of the meeting room.

His exchanges were very productive. He learned that the planet was home to close to twelve billion individuals. He was also learning the number system as it was happening. He was surprised to learn that there seemed to only be about ten language variations. That was much fewer than the two hundred and fifty that existed on Earth. The difference in population seemed to be proportional to the larger size of Anura and the smaller size of its beings.

From everything the team was learning it appeared that Anura technologically was only about fifty years behind Earth in its technology. The other significant difference was that Earth was roughly twenty nine percent land and seventy one percent water where it appeared that Anura was twenty percent land and eighty percent water. Another significant observation was that the structures on land all seemed to be industrial or military in nature and all homes seemed to be in the sea or in the fresh water that pock marked a great deal of the land.

By the end of the day Joe was once again exhausted from trying to understand what was similar to Earth and what was different.

He gathered the team and was surprised that the room was now overflowing.

Linda introduced the new comers.

She first introduced the lead linguist, Lillian Trundle, who said that she was impressed with the progress that had been made in only two days. She hoped that she and her linguistic partner Bao Zhao could get into the thick of things and make as much progress that had been made so quickly.

Then she introduced McMillan McClain an astronomer who had asked to be called Mack.

Mack stood up and said that it would take him a couple of days to get over the shock of having been thrown into his longtime dream of being able to study a faraway galaxy and a solar system in such a galaxy. He found it hard to believe that he had stepped into a chamber on Earth and stepped out to be met with the famous Tom Hall. The only embarrassment he had was that he had stepped out in the nude to be greeted by Tom holding a bathrobe.

Linda then introduced the person who looked like she was too young to buy an alcoholic drink in any country, Mia O'Reilly.

Mia stood smiled and said that she had aged enough on her trip to the Cosmos Odessey that she would welcome a good glass of Guinness stout. She then smiled and said that she was quite pleased that it had been Linda handing her the bathrobe.

Tom laughed and said that he had tried to stay for her arrival to properly welcome her but had been kicked out.

Mia nodded at him and said that she had been sent to be the team's devil advocate which meant she would be asking countless questions that would most likely irritate everyone including the famous Tom Hall. Her role was to break the standard thought process and cause everyone to look and think about what they were learning in a new light. She shook her head and said that after observing the team at work she had already stepped into a world that was new to her.

Finally, Linda introduced a person that looked like a young Santa Claus, Mack Finnegan

He stood up, smiled, and said that he had been pulled from his bed, given ten minutes to dress and then rushed by General Delaney the person he worked for to the unit referred to as the Door. The question he had managed to ask before rudely being told to get undressed and then pushed totally nude into the center of the enclosure was, "were am I going?" The answer I got occurred almost instantaneously when I was met by Tom handing me my robe. I want to thank him for at least telling me that I was in another galaxy and another solar system and that he had no idea who I was or what my role was to be.

I am an analyst of infrastructure. I recognize manufacturing facilities, weapons, and missile technology so if you are in need of a snoop to look in those areas I am the person to do it. I have the ability to look through camouflage and recognized the shapes that are being hidden.

Joe welcomed the five and said that during their "evening" meal he would ask each of the Odessey team to introduce themselves and share what they had learned so far.

The meal was going very well. Mia had just finished asking if any of the other planets had any signs of life when alarms went off.

Yara's voice announced that they had picked up an incoming missile that seemed to be coming from another planet. She stated that it did not seem to be aimed at the Cosmos but rather at the planet. She asked what action should she take.

Joe took a bite of his hamburger, jumped up and ran for the control room.

204

22

Jamaican Sun-the Grey of the Cell

Amber had just commented that they were enjoying the good life when Amanda, who was laying on her stomach and looking up the shore to where the refreshment cabana was located said that they might not be enjoying it much longer. Amber turned in her chair to look where Amanda was furtively pointing. There were three men and two women in dark suits walking out in their direction.

Amber looked around, stood up and began running down the beach toward a boat marina located in that direction. She felt like she was getting away as she ran. She then realized that her sister had not followed. She figured she would first make her escape and then worry about Amanda who she realized had not moved.

Amanda shook her head as she watched Amber running away. She figured that there was nowhere to run. The authorities had found them when she had been sure that she and Amber's tracks were well hidden. She wondered what had given away their location. She sat up as the five arrived where she was laying. They displayed their badges and let her know that she was under arrest. She was given the choice of coming with them and being flown back to the US or she would be arrested and held in a local jail until she could be extradited.

She stood up and asked if she was going to be handcuffed. She was told that it would be better for all of them if she just walked with them back to their vehicle. She picked up her towel and beach bag and walked with them to an unmarked van. She was handed a coverall to put on and then helped into the back of the van. She was then hand cuffed to a ring by her seat.

The van left the parking lot and drove for about five minutes and stopped. When the doors in back open she looked at Amber, smiled and asked her how her run had been.

Amber shook her head and said that she was greeted by two men who had arrested her and given her a choice. She said that she was glad that she had made the same choice of going to the US. She then asked where they were being taken but got the reply that they had no clue where they would be going until they got in the air.

Jorge was surprised to get a call from the CIA to let him know that they had apprehended the two saboteurs and had been instructed to take them directly to Lakland where they would be questioned and then arraigned. He called Doug and asked him to prepare two holding cells and to have a security detail to meet the incoming flight with the two saboteurs.

After he hung up, Jerry walked in and shared that he had been informed that he was to join the prosecutor that was arriving from DC to question the two to see if they would cooperate and identify their handler.

That evening they both joined Doug and his security team when the plane carrying the two arrived. The two women in dark blue overalls were led off the plane and remanded to Doug's custody with the instructions that the President wanted the two to be treated like the heinous criminals that they were and that their looks belied their cruelty.

Jorge was surprised by the instructions but he too was surprised at the cruelty that the two would have sown had it not been for Joe's insistent focus on finding all the bombs. He listened as Doug said that he would make sure the two would regret what they had done. Jorge looked at Doug and said that there should be no bruises.

That evening after he got home, he received a personal call from Lacey asking him to participate in the inquiry of the two saboteurs and make every effort to learn who their handlers were. She wanted the two to get the full benefit of being in prison for the rest of their lives but what she wanted even more was to track down the people that had enabled them.

Jorge agreed to do some digging and he would get back to her as soon as he had something.

The next day the prosecutor that the President had assigned to the case arrived. She was a surprise to Jorge as he had not been given hint who it might be. He learned that the prosecutor, Inés Alamilla was a lawyer that Lacey had on her staff.

Inés was surprised to be greeted by two Generals. She was escorted by them to the office of General Jorge Martinez. There she was offered something to drink. She listened as General Martinez suggested that he and General Delaney bring her up to speed on the details of the case against the two saboteurs and anyone associated with them.

Jorge asked Inés to call him by the name all of his friends called him and suggested that she refer to his best friend General Delaney as Jerry. He then took the cloth that was covering a long board that had several smaller graphics and data. He pointed to the picture of the USS Cosmos Odessey and said that the ship had been renamed by President McAdam. Jorge explained that 240 bomblets had been found and had been set up as booby traps. He went on to explain that the ships contingent was made up of six people and each person had six bombs directly aimed at them. He highlighted the one exception for the one bomb situated in the spacesuit helmet that would have killed the individual wearing the helmet. He went on to state that the remaining bombs had been set up so they would maim the individual by blowing off feet or hands or blowing up beneath their seat. The remaining bombs had been attached to the critical components of the ship.

He then pointed the number of destructive computer commands that had been inserted into the computer programing of every control computer on the ship.

He made the point that the two saboteurs that were in custody had implemented both bomb placement and computer code alteration.

Inés had been taking notes as Jorge talked. She had been told by the President that she was going to be surprised at the thoughtless and cruel nature of the two persons she was being sent to prosecute. She had been told that she had been chosen for the lead role in handling the prosecution because she would not be swayed by the good looks of the two who had carried out the sabotage and she would understand the cruelty that the two had willfully displayed. She thought she had been prepared for the case until she listened to Jorge.

She then followed the location of all bomb placements as the general made a point of taking her through every picture that was displayed. When he finally completed his presentation, she looked at the clock behind him and realized that he had been continuously talking for more than three hours and she had filled her pad with the notes she had been taking. She had not expected such a clear documentation of the situation and she now understood the Presidents comment about the fact that she was about to be surprised. She was also glad the President had suggested that she determine how many people she would need on her staff to handle the size of the case she expected would be surfaced.

Jerry smiled and said that now she understood how hard it was for him to get a word in edgewise when Jorge was talking. He suggested that they have lunch and then he would give her the background on the two women who worked for the company that had managed the redesign of the Cosmos Odessey.

Inés asked if they could have lunch brought in. She was after a small salad, some fruit yogurt, and a banana. She said that she was so overwhelmed that she could not really think about eating.

Jerry nodded and welcomed her to the club. Both he and Jorge had discussed wanting to shoot the two but had decided letting them rot in prison would be the more appropriate action. He went on to say that the two of them really wanted to go up the chain and find all the perpetrators and the instigating person who was at its source.

Inés said she was beginning to understand their feelings. She too wanted to get to the top and take action against those at the top. She asked if the two of them had the means of doing so.

Jorge shook his head and said that he did not have an organization to do so but between he, Jerry and the base's security Chief they had the means to do so. Their only limit was that they needed to keep it as legal as possible so that when they discovered the who, she would have the ammunition that would stand up in court. They had tracked down the location of the two saboteurs and had then let the President determine how the two would be brought back for trial and who would do the prosecution.

Inés nodded and said that she was beginning to understand why the President had chosen her to be the one to initiate the prosecution. She said that she did not care how the two of them followed the trail but when they were close to treeing the coon, she wanted to be the hound doing the barking.

She smiled when General Delaney barked and said that he too had grown up hunting raccoons in the middle of the night and had listened to many coon hounds barking at the coon and the best hounds had always been the females.

She nodded and said that she was of Spanish decent but had grown up in the center of Iowa and had spent many a night hiking through the woods with her father as they followed the sounds of their hunting dogs. She smiled and added that she wanted to follow the sounds of the President's two Generals as they tracked down their prey. She said that the President had her faith in their ability.

Lunch arrived and after they had all served themselves, Jerry stood up and turned the large board around. He had arranged three charts that described what he knew and where they planned to go next to find the leaders of the sabotage. The first chart showed the organization chart of the organization that had modified the Doorship and transformed it into the Cosmos Odessey.

He pointed to the person who directly managed the two saboteurs and added that he thought the guy was clueless about what the two had been doing. He had hired the two on the recommendation of the FBI contact that was responsible for giving the two top secret clearances.

He then highlighted the chain of command in the FBI and said that the person who had provided the hire recommendation was also most likely not the individual responsible for the two having top secrete clearances because the clearances were issued several years prior. The two had been working for another contractor that was doing work in an upcoming nuclear reactor plant.

Our hunt stops there because we need to get the guy at the FBI in our sights to give us the next tree where the next raccoon is hiding. Then we need to see if there is another raccoon beyond that.

Inés had only eaten a few bites of her salad. She now stopped to peel her banana and as she took her first bite she asked how she could help.

We need to see if the two we are holding can be made to give up the person who helped them get assigned to the work going on with the Cosmos Odessey.

Inés nodded and said that she would use taking the death sentence off the table as a bargaining chip if the two would give up the FBI contact. She added that she would not mention the fact that the number of premeditated murder plans, the maiming and personal injury charges would put them both in prison for thirty five to forty years.

Jorge shook his head and said it was a sad state of affairs that the two would not hang from the gallows.

Jerry laughed and asked what century Jorge was living in. He looked at Inés and said that the only reason he put up with him was because he grilled a mean steak and had promised to do so that evening. He then asked Inés if she were willing to put up with the two of them and their wives for the evening.

Inés replied that she would love to have dinner with the two of them and get to meet the women who put up with them. She asked if they had accommodations where she could get a quick shower and few moments to get ready. She asked what the dress code happened to be at these dinners.

Jorge apologized for not having been courteous enough to let her get situated before overwhelming her with the details of the sabotage.

He then said that he would be in jeans and a sports shirt and that dinner would be at six thirty.

23

<u>Planet Drako</u>

Joe came running into the control room and took his seat. He looked over at Yara and asked how long they had until the rocket reached its target.

H³ commented that the Odessey was not the target.

Yara replied that the rocket was headed straight toward the most populated section of Anura and they had roughly twenty minutes before it hit.

Joe gave her the command to immediately blow up the rocket.

Yara replied in the affirmative and pushed the button for the first laser. It fired and hit the missile about twenty feet from its nose. What followed seemed like the flowering of a fourth of July Chrysanthemum explosion that broke into a spherical pattern of colored stars and left a trail of sparks. The missile had been filled with a host of mini bombs meant to explode in the air and rain down shrapnel on the area below.

Almost immediately a signal came up from Anura with an offering of seaweed.

Joe replied with his face in a smile.

Joe looked over to where Mia was standing and said that she now had the answer to her question if there was another planet with intelligent beings.

Mia nodded and said that they were smart but evidently were not friendly, very strategic nor intelligent.

H^3 said that he had been able to get pictures of the beings on the fifth planet. He put it up on the main screen and everyone let out a gasp.

Lydia shook her head and said that the beings on Anura were very gentle looking as compared to what she took to be a dinosaur of some kind that had lost its tail.

H^3 put up a silhouette of a six foot tall man and a silhouette of the beings on the fifth planet. The fifth planet being silhouette was twice the height of the man. It had feet and legs that seemed to be built to be running. The arms were rather short for the size of the beings who had what appeared to be claws that could close into a ball but did not have an opposing thumb. The neck made up a third of the height of the being and the other two thirds was evidently the organ cavity that was shorter than the legs. The exterior "skin" was made up of what appeared to be scales that were black at their center and got lighter in color and then were bordered with a thin red edging.

Samantha commented that she had always wondered what dinosaurs would have looked like if they had become intelligent beings. She pointed at the screen and said that they would look like the beings on the planet Draco. She added that they looked formidable and treacherous.

Joe nodded and said that until they were able to communicate with the beings on the fifth planet and learn the name they called it, Draco would be the name.

The dominant war lord on Wŭ, Scorp, known for his ferocious temper let out a deep throated hiss as the missile he had launched to obliterate the largest population of Anurans exploded long before it reached its destination. He was furious and wanted to know why he did not know of the Anuran's new defense capability. He had waited until to fire the assault missile until he was sure that the Anurans had used their only missile. He had expected an easy annihilation of billions of beings he had grown up despising even though he had never met any of them in his life.

He had battled and conquered all of his adversaries on Wŭ and was now looking to develop the capability to travel to the seventh planet and conquer the weak looking beings who had tried to establish communication many times.

For a great deal of time, he had his scientist communicating with the planet that he learned was called Anura. They had gleaned much information from the continuous communication. He was amazed that, beings as small as they could have enough brain power to develop almost the same technology as his scientist had developed.

He again asked how the capability that had been demonstrated could have been missed.

The leader of the missile team cringed and said that there was no Anuran intelligence that described the ability to blow up the missile. He went on to say that the light that was seen hitting the missile did not originate from the planet.

This caught Scorp by surprise he immediately asked if Wǔ was under attack and was reassured that it was not. He then commanded that the source and location of the weapon that had so easily destroyed his missile be determined. Next he asked when the next missile would be ready to launch and was assured it was being moved to the launch pad as he spoke.

Joe had asked that the fifth planet get closely monitored and that a satellite get launched that would go around it and capture pictures, electronic signals, and any other information the team could analyze.

Darian said the he would launch several satellites so that they could get a relatively fast understanding of what it looked like and how developed it might be. He said he was going to first locate the origin of the missile launch.

Mack said that he was going to flesh out the solar system they were in so they could get a better understanding of its lay out and the state of the twelve planets.

Lilian said that she was interested in getting any communications that might be going on between the two planets. This might speed up their ability to set up more robust communications.

Bao shook his head and said that it was going to be very interesting learning Anuran or Frog and Draconia or dinosaur and figure out both languages. He said he was with Samantha about how intelligent dinosaurs would have looked. The beings on Draco seemed very fierce and aggressive. He wondered if their language would reflect that fierceness.

Mia had been quiet for a while then she asked why the Draconian's had chosen this particular time to launch their rocket and what target the rocket had been going to hit.

H^3 said that he bet that when the Anuran's launched their rocket at the Cosmos, the Draconians, if they knew that the Anurans had only one missile capable of reaching Dracon, had most likely figured they would have a tremendous advantage if they hit a population center with their missile. He then put up the trajectory of the missile and the projection of where it would hit. He pointed out that it would have hit the densest population center on Anura. He went on to add that the intensity of the missile explosion would have devastated an area that would have resulted in almost two billion Anurans being killed or very badly injured.

Tom spoke up and said that he recommended that along with the satellites to learn more about the Draconians, they should position several laser weapons closer to that planet so that if another launch occurred the missile could be destroyed immediately upon reaching space.

Linda nodded and said that she agreed with Tom but she thought that a more impactful demonstration would be to destroy the rocket on its launch pad before it was launched.

Joe smiled and said that he would never play poker with her because she was brutal in her attack. He then asked H^3 to get the coordinates for the missile launch facility and then pin point the base of the launch pad. He was going to take Linda's suggestion and as soon as a missile was placed on the launch pad he wanted Yara to use their lasers to knock it over.

Joe then ordered the Cosmos to position itself half way between the two planets but not in the orbital path of the sixth planet.

Mia asked if there was any life on the sixth planet.

Joe shook his head, said that he had no idea and asked Mack to get footage of the sixth planet and determine if there was life on it.

He looked over at Tom and asked him to prepare a message describing what had happened and send it back through the Hole. He commented that it had only been three days but he felt that they had been gone for a year. He added that he wondered if time passed differently in this part of the universe.

Mia laughed and said she didn't want competition in being a devil's advocate and that it was her role to ask the questions.

Jorge was informed when the information missile appeared over Lakland. He had not been expecting it and wondered what Joe and his team were experiencing and if they had made any progress in communicating with the beings on the seventh planet.

He was captivated by the fact that on the first mission of the Cosmos Odessey a planet with intelligent life had been found. This was really the icing on the cake.

The success of having traversed the Universe to a totally different galaxy and a unique solar system was success at the highest level. To be communicating with a technically advanced civilization was not only icing but so fascinating that it was hard for him to wait on what the linguistic team and the technical analysis would surface as additional learning.

He went to the Cosmos Odessey control center to be there when the most recent message module was activated. When the message was activated it simply said that it was the last message rocket that would be sent through the hole and that they should look in the Door module for a full report.

Jorge knew immediately that another revolutionary breakthrough had happened. He went to the Door operating center and asked what had been received.

The technicians said they had received an organic crystal and they were working on decoding the noncovalent interactions in the organic crystal that seemed to be manipulating the light going through it.

Jorge suggested that they match the interactions with the alphabet and see if a message would materialize.

As soon as that association was made and deciphered by the computer the lengthy message sent by someone on the Cosmos Odessey was deciphered.

Jorge asked if someone in the lab knew how to reply using the same approach.

As the message ended, a smiley face was shown on the screen and the instructions of how to program an organic crystal appeared. It said that the equipment to produce a fresh organic crystal with an embedded message was stored in the cabinet labeled, "Crystal Magic." Then another smiley face came up followed by "Tom."

Jorge could not help but laugh because the mad scientist that he had recruited to develop the Door technology and who had gone on to develop the Hole technology had once again provided another leap forward in being able to use the Door for communication as well as to transport people and live food.

Tom waited eagerly outside of the Door module to see if he would get a response from the team back at Lakland. He was about to give up when a crystal module appeared at the center of the Door transport area. He picked it up and by passing a beam of light through it he was able to read the simple reply, "We have received your message. We congratulate you on another breakthrough and we appreciate you leaving the equipment that allowed us to reply immediately.

Tom took the crystal and returned to the Cosmos control room. He held up the crystal and announced that he and Linda had been able to create an organic crystal with which he could send and receive messages via the Door. He added that they now had an ample supply of missiles that could be used for more than sending messages.

H^3 shook his head and asked when Tom had the time to do that development and get the equipment needed to imbed a message into the crystal.

Linda laughed and said that the two of them had been working on that capability before they had achieved the Hole breakthrough. It had been on their to do list since the Door breakthrough and it had taken them longer than they anticipated. She went over to Tom and gave him a kiss on the forehead and smiled as his face turned as red as his hair.

23 Planet Drako

24

<u>Obligate Bipeds</u>

Mack excitedly called out that he had proof that beings of obligate terrestrial bipedalism populated the sixth planet. He added that they were not as advanced as those on the other two planets but they definitely were on their way. He said that it appeared that they were in the process of switching between being nomadic hunter-gatherers to becoming farmers. He noted that they were about where ancient Egypt had been some twelve thousand years ago.

Darian laughed and said that he was sure that the beings on the sixth planet were not obligated to any terrestrial he knew. This did not get the laugh he had been hoping for.

Mia asked how it was possible that three distinctly different species developed intelligence in the same solar system on three adjacent planets and that each of their civilizations were making progress similar to what Earth had experienced. She said that to her it seemed very improbable.

Joe shook his head and said he had no idea what it meant other than they had been very lucky not to have gone through the first and second Holes. He wondered what they would find in the other two Holes they had chosen not to go through.

He said that as soon as they finished dealing with what they currently had found he would recommend going through the other two Holes to see if anything similar was waiting for them there. He was now wondering if Earth was the lone planet in a solar system that had intelligence and whether other solar systems were more prolific than the one he had been born into. He went on to say that all three planets in this solar system were located in the Goldilocks zone that was much broader than the zone that Earth and Mars were in.

Darian spoke up and asked if Goldilocks had faced the three dinosaurs or the three frogs or the three bipedal beings. He only knew the story of Goldilocks and the three bears.

Mack asked if he could get a couple of satellites to circle the sixth planet so that he could dig more deeply into its evolving society.

H^3 commented that Drako was the smallest of the three, the sixth or Neo as he was calling it after the Neolithic age on Earth was slightly larger and Anura was the largest. He went on to add that the land mass decreased as each of the planets increased in size.

Lydia said that they should try to find out what the beings on each planet called their world before they became like the Spaniards, English, French and the Netherlands and renamed the different parts of Earth based on their own culture.

Bao spoke up and said that the images and the writing that he had seen on Drako seemed very similar to Mandarin and that he figured the writing system would be logographic and that the language would be a tonal language.

He added that the Chinese had four unique tones that included flat, rising, falling then rising, and falling. He went on to say that there were several varieties of Mandarin that included Wu, Xiang, Min, Hakka, and Gan. He wondered if something similar might be present on Drako.

He was eager to establish communication with the beings there so he could penetrate deeper into their language.

Lilian nodded and shared the fact that her initial understanding of the language on Anura was also a tonal language but seemed to be of a different pattern than Chinese Mandarin. She was thinking it was more like the Indian Sanskrit alphabet, the varṇamālā, and the sounds that she had so far heard were a mix of nasal and back of mouth sounds that had her thinking about the Sanskrit alphabet and the sounds associated with it.

She then asked if there would be a way to listen to the spoken language of the people on Neo. If it could be arranged then they would have three languages to study and the team waiting back on Earth would have their hands full trying to develop a comprehensive understanding of three languages.

H^3 said that they might be able to position a satellite that had enough sensitivity to capture the voices of the beings conversing on Neo. The satellites certainly had the capability to get very good visuals and they might be able to pick up sounds.

On Drako, Scorp had been threatening his scientific team with torture and cutting of some of their digits as he tried to get them to give him more strategic information about the strange vessel that they had finally found floating between Wǔ and the planet Anura.

The vessel did not look very formidable and he was sure that it was now close enough that his missile would obliterate it before the beings on it had a chance to defend themselves. He was informed that the missile was now in position and could be launched at his command.

This was a missile he had commissioned to obliterate Anura but now he would use it to eliminate a new enemy. The strange vessel seemed so fragile to him, not something solid like what he was about to hit them with.

He decided that he would go to the launch site and be the one to launch the solid bomb missile, the most powerful that had so far been built. He felt that he should be the one to lead Wǔ to defeat the Aliens that had intruded in his realm.

H³ had been monitoring the only missile launch site on the fifth planet and let Joe know that a rocket was getting ready to launch.

Joe nodded and gave Lydia the order to destroy the rocket before it took off. He instructed her to knock the rocket over but not hit the missile itself. He was not looking to have it explode, he only wanted to demonstrate the fact that they knew what was going on and had the means of stopping the launch.

Aliens We

On Wǔ, Scorp pushed the launch button and almost simultaneously a beam from the sky flashed and hit the tail fins. He watched in horror as the giant rocket seemed to slowly fall toward him as it fired it first stage thrust engines. He was in complete shock when suddenly there was an unbelievable flash and then the world went black as the rocket blew up and the heat wave and explosion forces erased the building he was in.

Joba had been monitoring the entire sequence and was amazed at the size of the blast as the rocket accelerated horizontally and crashed into the launch control station. The cameras went black. She tried other cameras in the area but they were all inoperative. She then ordered flying drones to get a picture of the area and was surprised to learn that the area of destruction was a huge two hundred mile circle of ash where all life had been eliminated. She was glad that it was an area that was sparsely populated but none the less more than one hundred thousand Wǔan's had lost their lives.

H^3 had put the entire episode on the large screen and those on the Odessey watched as the missile fired its engines just as the laser fired by Lydia hit the bottom of the missile. The hit cause the bottom of the missile to get moved out and the missile was almost horizontal as its engines accelerated it towards the only structure close to the launch site. When it hit the building the explosion that occurred cause a mushroom cloud to rise up and out into space as it spread in a circle outward and flattened everything for more than two hundred miles.

Joe shook his head and let out a groan. He looked around at the faces in the control room and knew that they were all as surprised as he was about what had just happened. He wondered why the Draconian's were so determined to kill people that they built a missile that was powerful enough to spew the destruction shown on the screen. He then shook his head as he thought about the use of the atomic bomb that was dropped on Hiroshima. He realized that just by looking in the mirror he would see another race very much like the Draconians.

He asked Bao to try and communicate with the beings on Darco. He wanted to see if he could put an end to their hostile attempts.

Joba knew that she was for the moment in control but soon she would literally be fighting for her life as Scorp's enemies moved to take his place. She had strong support and hoped she could be as ruthless as those that would be ready to eliminate her. She also needed to deal with the Aliens that had demonstrated the power to reach down and destroy the most powerful weapon ever produced on Wŭ.

The communications technician excused himself but announced that a signal was coming in from the vessel they had targeted.

She turned to look at the screen and saw one of the most hideous looking beings standing and holding up one of his very weak looking arms with an open hand. She was surprised that like her he stood upright, had no snout to speak of but had two eyes and an opening that she took to be a mouth that seemed too small to be used the way she used hers to tear the flesh off the bone.

She wondered if the open hand meant the same as it did on Wǔ. She raised her hand to indicate that she had no weapon. She watched as the being dropped its hand and then pointed to a diagram that she instantly recognized as her star system. He pointed at her planet and raised both hands. She hissed out Wǔ. She was surprised to hear the being hiss Wǔ back at her. The being then pointed at the seventh planet and she hissed out Anura and heard the hissing response. It was clear to her that the being was trying to establish communication with her. She looked over her shoulder and called the Wǔan who was the best with all the different languages on Wǔ. She pointed at him and hissed out Juss.

Joe signaled for Lillian and Boa to join him. He then said their name with a Wǔan hiss.

He listened as the person who now seemed in charge hissed their two names back. He then made a bow, turned, and stepped out of the camera sight leaving Lillian and Boa.

Joba nodded her head as she understood that the discussion was over and she turned and walked away and left Juss standing by himself.

Lillian began to use sign language and asked Boa to bring their objects kit that had geometric objects and a variety of shapes that they could use to begin to capture the sounds for that the Wǔan on the planet would make.

Once Joba was out of the camera, she immediately put what were now her forces to full alert. She was not going to allow the opposition time to mount any subversive action. She was going to arrest the strongest of the lot and put them into detention until she was sure she could maintain control. She had come to the conclusion that she would focus on maintaining power and the focus on improving the condition of Wŭ versus worrying about conquering other worlds. She was satisfied with the power she exerted on Wŭ.

Joe looked around the room and asked if everyone had enough excitement for one day. He was ready to call it a day. He looked at Lydia and asked her if she would join him for a walk around the Cosmos.

Once they were walking, he asked her how she was feeling about what had happened. She replied that she was shocked by the devastation that she had been a apart of. She had only been planning to topple the rocket. The fact that it had been launched at the moment that the laser hit its base resulted in devastation that she had not imagined. She wondered how many Wŭans had died.

Joe nodded and remined her that she was following his orders and that neither of them had expected to create such havoc.

Linda and Tom were walking behind them. Linda spoke up and reminded him that the rocket was being launched to attack them. Tom added that H^3 had verified that if there had been additional missiles they no longer existed. The entire area around the missile site was now bare. He went on to say that it would give them time to establish communication with the beings on all three planets.

Lydia commented that she agreed with communicating with the beings on two of the planets but the beings on the third planet were probably not ready to have Aliens show up.

Linda said that she agreed and if they did show up they would start the long history of Aliens coming down from the sky. Similar to the ones on Earth. She smiled and asked who Joe thought those Aliens might have been.

Joe replied that he figured those Aliens had been explores that like those on the Cosmos Odessey had visited Earth at about the same period of time that the beings on the sixth planet were living. He was not about to allow anyone to interrupt the progress of those beings.

H^3 and Samantha caught up with the four and said that he was ready for a vacation.

Joe laughed and reminded him that they were only on day three of their mission but he too felt that it had been a long journey so far.

234

25

<u>Hot on the Trail</u>

Lyle had invited Caitlyn, the newly arrived addition to his unit, out to lunch and was enjoying listening to her as she shared all the gossip that was going around the circles of her chain of coworkers.

Caitlyn had as many years in the organization as he but had been in internal affairs. She had been transferred parallel into his division with the promise that it was a step to a promotion. She had asked him who above her rating was retiring and he had truthfully answered that he had no clue.

That response seemed to have triggered a continuous flow of information about what she had heard that was going on somewhere in the FBI, CIA, and DEA. He recognized that extent of her network but it was much better than his. He figured that she would do very well and get that promotion she was seeking.

He was passively listening until Caitlyn asked him if he had heard about the secret group that the President had sent to apprehend some bad guys in the Bahamas. They had captured them and whisked them off to some secrete location. That was when he had almost dropped his fork. He asked her when that had happened and found out that it had only been two days since she had been given that information.

She laughed and added that the spooks were even invisible to the normal group of spooks and when she tried to find out more she found out that whatever had happened never happened.

At Lakland, Jorge, Jerry and Doug had put all their resources to work. Jorge was working closely with Inés to extract useful information from the two saboteurs.

Inés said that she really hated to make any deal with the two but she understood the need to get all the information from them as possible. The President had made it clear that she was to use all means to identify the people at the top who had facilitated putting the two into the position where they could do their work. She made the point that she did not care what organization or what level the individual held, she wanted the culprit identified and arrested.

Amber and Amanda had been in separate holding cells that were in two different locations on the base for two days. No one spoke to them. They were fed three meals a day but were in total isolation.

Amanda knew that the two of them were in deep trouble and that so far they had not been offered any legal representation. She decided that was the first thing that she would demand. Once she had that she would lie to her lawyer and say that she was being framed and that she was innocent and had nothing to do with what she was being accused of. She hoped that Amber was holding up and thinking along the same lines.

Amber was in her holding cell wishing she could talk with Amanda so they could decide how to handle that deep hole they were in.

Inés suggested that they first set the two up in two separate rooms so they could question them separately. Then they would put the two together for a third questioning session. She handed out the questions that she was planning to ask to the two Generals. She asked if they had any specific questions that they wanted to add.

Jorge looked at Jerry and said that Inés was not planning to ask whether the two preferred to be shot or be hung.

Jerry smiled and replied that he wanted to add the gas chamber to the choices they could choose from.

Inés shook her head and said that she took their exchange to mean that she had the right set of questions. She knew the two were very serious about finding who the next person up the line was.

Doug, the fourth person in the room had been quiet. He spoke up and asked what kind of deal was she willing to make to get the two to give them useful information.

Inés nodded and said that she would offer to spare them their lives and the possibility of parole after serving whatever sentence they might get for attempted murder, serious bodily harm, and destruction of government property.

Doug shook his head and said that it seemed too generous for what the two had tried to do.

Inés nodded and said that she agreed with him but she was going to have more than twenty charges against each of them and each charge would carry between five to seven years each. That would stack up to be between one hundred to one hundred forty years of jail time. The possibility of parole would happen after thirty years of good behavior.

Doug nodded and said he understood the need to get those who had facilitated putting the two in position but it still made him angry that the two would get off so lightly. He felt like they should somehow suffer more.

Jorge asked Doug to have the two brought to the interview rooms. He suggested letting them sit by themselves for the next couple of hours. The four of them could go to the officers club for lunch and then they could begin the interviews.

Inés said that sounded like a good approach. She wanted to take a moment and send an update to the President and then she would be ready for lunch.

Jorge asked her to say hello to Lacey for him. He then got up and let the way out of his office. He stopped for a moment to let his support know that they were all going to the officers club for lunch.

After lunch Doug left to manage his team that was following up some leads that he had from the background check of the two women. He said that he had identified their previous employer and was following up to see if that employer had any involvement.

Inés had selected to begin the interview process with Amber the twin she assessed as the weaker of the two. She led the way in to the meeting room and was followed by the two generals. She sat down, introduced herself, General Jorge Martinez, and General Gerald Delaney. She was about to describe the interview process and how Amber could cooperate and benefit when suddenly General Delaney stood up, leaned across the table, and slammed his hand down in front of Amber.

Jerry had discussed what he was going to do with Jorge. He was going to play the bad ass and hope to scare the living day lights out of the two. When he stood up he saw the surprised look on Amber's face and when he slammed his hand down on the table in front of her she cringed and pushed back in her chair.

"You're lucky that I was able to keep the lynch mob that is outside from breaking in and dragging you to the gasoline soaked wood pile they set up outside to burn you at the stake," he shouted at her while he was leaning as close to her as he could.

Inés had not been expecting the General's outburst but she could see by General Martinez's relaxed expression that he had been expecting it. She looked at Amber's face and knew that it had the effect that she was sure the Generals wanted it to have.

She assumed a stern tone and asked General Delaney to please sit down, assume a more professional manner or she would have him removed. She leaned toward Amber and in a confidential tone stated that now she now understood how difficult it was for a lawyer to handle the military in the situation that she faced. She added that the military took care of their own and she had messed with the two branches of the military.

Amber shook her head in agreement as Inés sat back between the two Generals and quietly shared with her how difficult it was to work with the two. She asked if there was really a wood pile outside.

Inés shook her head and said that she was not sure about being burned at the stake, but she reinforced the fact that both she and her sister were currently the ones that were being accused of heinous crimes that would lead to their death sentences by lethal chemical injections. She watched as Amber's hands trembled and tears appeared in her eyes.

Inés then said that if Amber cooperated and identified those that had instructed she and her sister about what to do, how to do it and had supplied the bomb materials she would make sure that the death penalty was removed from consideration.

Amber asked if she could ask for a lawyer.

Inés replied that she could but then she would not remove the death penalty from consideration and would make sure the jury understood the heinous nature of all the bombs that had been placed. She added that she was sure the jury would react very similar to General Delaney and find her guilty which would lead shortly after to the lethal injection needle being pushed into the vein in her arm.

Inés had slowly removed her jacket and had run her finger up her arm to the vein on her left arm as she enacted the needle being administered. This had not been planned but she liked the lead that the Jerry had given her and she could see that it was having an effect on Amber.

She then looked at the guard standing by the meeting room door and asked if he would bring in a glass for each of them and a pitcher of ice water.

After a moment's hesitation she asked her first question.

Do you have the name of the person who got you hired to be on the startup team for the equipment up on the Cosmos Odessey?

Amber was quiet for a moment and said that she had a name but she wanted to make sure that the deal that was being offered would also cover Amanda.

The question let Inés know that she was going to get what she was after. She nodded and said that cooperating would cover Amanda. She then asked if Amber would feel better if the two of them were interviewed together.

Amber shook her head up and down vigorously indicating that she wanted it to happen.

Inés looked at the guard by the door and asked that he bring Amanda into the room.

A few minutes later Amanda was led into the room by one guard and another guard brought in another chair and put it next to the one Amber was sitting in.

This time Jorge stood and quietly introduced everyone. He then leaned toward the two and said that he hoped that together they would willingly cooperate and save themselves from the death penalty. He smiled and added that if they answered the questions they were about to be asked truthfully he would make sure that while they were in his custody they would remain together and safe from retaliation by anyone in the military.

Amanda asked why they were not represented by a lawyer.

Amber replied that if they asked for a lawyer they would face the risk of a death sentence but if they cooperated they would not face the death sentence.

Amanda put her hand on Amber's then looked across the table and asked if what her sister had shared was true.

Inés nodded and said that it was true.

Amanda was quiet for a moment and then asked what were the question they needed to answer.

The questioning commenced and three hours later the two were taken from the interview room and led back to a holding cell where they would be together.

Inés commented that she had never worked with two people that were so good at setting the interview scene as the two of them. She thanked them for having set things up so that they had been able to identify the on scene person that was directing the two, and the person in the FBI that had first contacted them. Now they needed to take the next step and break each of them so that they could continue to follow the trail. The two that she had the names for represented two steps up but she did not think the person in the FBI was the top and that there had to be someone higher.

Jorge nodded and said that both of them would continue to be available as she followed that trail. He would make sure that Doug took the local handler into custody and he would work with the President to apprehend the FBI contact. He reiterated that both he and Jerry would be in support during any interview process.

Inés smiled and said that they should give her a heads up on how they were going to play the bad General and the good General for each of the next interviews.

Jerry smiled and said that he was always the good General and Jorge was always the bad General.

Inés laughed and replied that as far as she could tell they were both devious Generals.

25 Hot on the Trail

26

<u>FBI Traitor</u>

Lyle found it hard to finish lunch. What Caitlyn had shared about spooks was that other spooks knew nothing about set off loud alarm bells. He decided that he needed to take some immediate vacation and decided to use some of the thirty days that he had accumulated and try to disappear for as long as possible.

He arranged with his boss to go to Vegas to do some gambling when in fact, he was going to hide much closer to home. He withdrew twenty thousand dollars cash from his bank account. He did this in five separate withdrawals so he would not trigger any bank alarms. He figured that he needed enough money to stay underground until things died down.

Once he had that money he used his credit card to buy a round trip ticket to Los Vegas. He had bought the tickets as a way to misdirect anyone trying to find him. He had no intentions of using the tickets. He had purposely gone to the Airport so that his face would show up there. He did a little shopping and then waited for his plane to be boarded. He gave his ticket to a standby and watched him board. He then threw up his hoody and made sure not to look at any cameras as he left the airport.

He drove his pickup out of the Dulles International Airport and headed north towards the New York State Finger Lakes. He had camped there several time in the past and figured that it was a good place to disappear until he was certain that he had not been fingered. He was careful to stay just below the speed limit.

As Lyle drove northward, Inés was asking the President to send her special team to apprehend FBI agent, Lyle Spencer and bring him in for questioning.

Lacey congratulated Inés for having made such quick progress.

Inés chuckled and said that much of the progress was due to two rather eccentric General's that had played good General and really bad General. The two had affected her and she had gotten into the action and threatened the twins with the death penalty.

Lacey asked where Inés wanted the FBI agent taken.

Inés suggested sending him to Lakland so he was out of the influence zone of the FBI and a place where he would personally feel isolated and vulnerable. She added that it also would let her enjoy an evening grill out at General Martinez's house.

Lacey laughed and said she understood because she had enjoyed several of the General's barbecues. She confirmed that agent Spencer would be delivered to Lakland as requested and she should say hello to her two favorite Generals.

That evening Inés shared her conversation she had with the President and the fact that she had arranged to have their wayward FBI agent delivered to Lakland.

Jorge nodded and said that she had earned another grilled steak dinner for keeping him from having to go to DC.

Inés laughed and admitted that was what she told the President she was after by having him brought to Lakland.

Jerry chuckled and asked what approach they should take.

Doug said that he would soften this agent up by having him slightly abused by a couple of his team members that were on the crazy side and had tattoos that made them look like Black Angel bikers.

Inés said that she wanted to make sure that they did not do anything illegal.

Doug shook his head and said that he would make sure they kept their actions at or below the misdemeanor assault charge level.

Inés said that she did not want to see any abuse marks.

Lyle drove all day and arrived at the Berry Patch campground where he had stayed several times. He paid for four days and then he figured he would move to another Finger lake after that. He rented a camp site that was the farthest in toward the back of the campground.

He had previously outfitted his pickup with a popup tent in the extra-long pickup that featured a full length bed on one side, a comfortable recliner that unfolded centered at the back under the rear window and a low style refrigerator powered by his pickup's power supply. He had enjoyed these features for several years and always got a good night's sleep after eating a chicken pot pie cooked over the camp site's grill or a nice grilled trout if he had been lucky at fishing.

Almost every time he had camped within a fifteen minute drive of the small mom and pop diner named, "You are Here," he had treated himself to a meal there. He drove there, went in, and ordered their sausage and barbecued ribs for dinner with mashed potato and green beans. He was especially looking forward to a slice of the coconut cream pie with a cup of hot chocolate for desert.

He was surprised when the owner's wife that was waiting on the tables remembered him and said that it had been a while and asked him where he was staying. Without thinking he answered her that he was staying at the Berry Patch and as soon as he had done so he regretted it. He decided to just enjoy the meal and not worry about the fact that he had been recognized. He was sure that she did not know his name or where he was from.

After a very satisfying and delicious dinner he returned to his campsite, parked his truck, popped up his tent, zipped the back entrance shut and got into his bed. He was ready for a good night's sleep. He felt that he would not easily be found.

As he fell asleep a dark green helicopter with a team of six flew over the camp ground where he had chosen to stay. The six had determined that he was not on the flight to Vegas and had then obtained a warrant and searched his house where they found pictures of his previous Finger Lake camping trips. One picture that clearly was a selfie that had Lyle standing in front of a restaurant with the sign, "You are Here" had given then the impression that it was a good place to eat and one where he might go. They had arranged to fly there and check to see if he had recently been there.

Aliens We

Mable was in the process of sweeping up and cleaning all the tables before closing when she heard a noise outside. She walked to the front window and watched as six people got out of a dark green helicopter and walked toward the entrance. She immediately thought of the movie where the secret agents all wore black suits. She watched as four men and two women entered the diner as if they were expecting to face some dangerous person. She let them know the diner was closed for the day.

The person in the lead pulled out a picture and asked her if she had seen him before.

Mable immediately recognized the man who had been in earlier. She asked who the six were. They each showed their badges that they wore on their belts. She noticed that they each were armed. She responded that the person in the picture had been in that evening for dinner and had said he was camping at the Berry Patch campground that was located about ten miles east of the diner.

She stood quietly as one of the agents looked at her phone and said she had located the place. The leader thanked her for the information and the six walked back to the helicopter and got in. Mable watched as after a few moments the helicopter powered up and rose into the dark night sky. She wondered what kind of trouble the person who had eaten dinner was in.

It took only a few moments for the helicopter to fly to the entrance of the Berry Patch campground. The team of six split so three went one way into the campground that was shaped somewhat like a large teardrop with the wide part of the tear at the far end. They had the license plate of the pickup they were looking for and slowly made their way on foot as they looked for the pickup. Most of the camps had a camper and a separate vehicle so it did not take long for the three of them to approach the lone pickup from both sides of the only a pickup parked by itself at a campsite.

After verifying the license plate and that there was no one in the cab, two of the six unzipped the back of the popup pickup tent and all six shined their lights in as the leader shouted out, "Lyle Spencer you are under arrest, come out with your hands up."

Lyle came wide awake when he heard his name called out. He sat bolt upright, put his hands over his eyes to shield them from the blinding light and swung his feet out of bed. He had led enough raids to know that he was most likely covered by several guns that were at the ready. He stood up in his underwear and asked if he could get dressed. He was told to step out to the ground and then they would have him get dressed.

Once dressed he was cuffed and put in the backseat of the pickup. He had one agent sitting to his right and one to his left. He could hear the other agents talking about how to proceed as he heard the tent lowered down so the back was flat.

He watched one of the agents get into the driver's seat and ask for the keys.

Aliens We

Lyle said he had he keys in his pocket and just pressing the start button would start the engine. Ten minutes after ten was the time that appeared on the digital clock read out on the radio console when the pickup engine started. He shook his head when he realized that he had only been asleep for an hour. He realized that whoever had sent the six person team out had acted swiftly and had the resources available to do so. He wondered how much hot water he was in and how much prison time might be in front of him.

When the pickup got to campground exit, Lyle saw what looked to him to be a black helicopter sitting with only a flare that was lighting up the area near the road. He wondered which of the agencies was taking him into custody.

He was taken and place in the helicopter and a few moments later two of the six agents got in and each sat to either side facing him. It was clear that the other four were going to take his truck to where ever it was bound. He took note that he and the two agents were being flown toward the west. An hour later they landed in the airport that he figured was the Buffalo Niagara International Airport. He took note that the place they landed was to a back corner of the airport where private jets parked. He was taken from the hilo and walked by his two escorts to an unmarked white jet and taken in and cuffed to a seat. He looked around the light tan interior and saw that it had six dark tan leather seats and there was a sleeping area in the back. A table located across from him held a bowl of fruit and a small vase with a clutch of yellow flowers.

Two pilots one a rather young looking female was the captain and an older grey haired pilot was her copilot.

When the two agents came on board, Lyle asked where he was being taken.

The larger and meaner looking of the two smiled and said that where was none of his concern but who they were turning him over to should be because he was being delivered into the hands of the meanest people he had ever dealt with.

The other agent laughed and said that if what he had done was true he would be lucky to live through the waterboarding.

Lyle was immediately alarmed by the attitude of the two.

Once the flight had taken off, one of the agents said he was going to catch some sleep. The other agent sat down at the table and peeled a succulent tangerine and a slowly ate each section. He smiled at Lyle and said that the fruit was delicious.

Lyle asked if by chance he might have one.

He watched as the agent slowly put another wedge of the tangerine in his mouth and slowly say, "No."

27

<u>Change of Command</u>

Joe brought the team together and posed a question that was on his mind. He asked if the team was ready to relinquish command of the Cosmos Odyssey and see if they could get another ship and try going into one of the first two Holes.

Tom shook his head and said that he had been working with the astronomy group and he suggested that instead of trying to go through one of the first two Holes they try a fourth location that seemed to have a solar system similar to the one that they had found in the third Hole but he added that he was all for moving on to another assignment.

Darian nodded and said that he was with Tom and ready to move on and let another team establish the relationships that needed to exist with the two different planets that they had established initial contact with.

Samantha added that she and Darian had discussed what they would do next and had both agreed that they would go wherever he and Lydia went.

Yara stood, walked over to the wall in the room, put her hand on it, looked around, then said that the Cosmos Odyssey was built by her homeland, Brasil, and she personally would like to stay with the Odessey.

H^3 spoke up and said that where Yara stayed he stayed.

He looked at Yara and said that it was great that she desired to stay because it would provide the leadership continuity needed. However, for her to stay on the Cosmos Odyssey, he would need to promote her to Captain. Her responsibilities would be to ensure the safety of the personnel on the Odessey and keep it in top condition.

He then said that he would promote H^3 to be the Odessey's Chief Scientific Officer at a similar but non command rank.

He added that he would make both positions formal and official before he left the Odessey.

He looked around at everyone and said that they were all explorers not the ones to establish interstellar relationships. He commented that interstellar politics, power relationships, economic trade relationships and the establishment of interstellar laws were all areas that were far removed from what the team had embraced and were really trained to do.

He then said that he was going to ask that another Doorship be refitted and become the next vessel with Hole transition capability. He was thinking of renaming the chosen Doorship to Cosmos Voyager and he would have it go through the next Hole that Tom and Linda recommended.

Back on Earth, Jorge was having lunch with Jerry when the thought of going out to the Cosmos Odyssey crossed his mind. He asked Jerry whether he was up to an official visit to the Odessey.

Jerry looked at Jorge to see if he was serious and then asked if he should wear his dress uniform.

Jorge laughed and asked if Jerry remembered how everyone was dressed when they came out of the Door enclosure. He then added that they were lucky that they had clothes that they had left behind when the Odessey was still Doorship One. He then suggested they go that afternoon and then return for a late dinner at his house.

Jorge called over to the base's Door team and asked them to send a communications module to the Odessey letting them know that he and General Delaney would be coming to the Odessey and to request that the team there have their outfits ready and that they keep the visit a surprise.

He then let Jimena know what he was doing and that he planned to return that evening and suggested that they go to the officers club for dinner.

The transfer to the Odessey went without a hitch. He and Jerry were met by the technicians, both of whom had been part of the Door team back on Earth and had been glad to grant him his request.

Once they were dressed he asked where Joe happened to be and was told that everyone was in the communication center that had become the unofficial control room and meeting center since the connection with the two planets had been established.

As they walked along the circumference of the Odessey, Jorge said that he had missed the walks that the two of them had been religious about taking every day when they were in the process of delivering Doors.

Jerry commented that it had always amazed him that he could be whisked from Earth to somewhere in the Solar system and now he had been whisked to some distant galaxy in the same instantaneous time.

Jorge replied that Tom had explained that coming through the Hole was actually a shorter distance than going through the Door some place in the Solar system because the Hole effectively folded the fabric of space and created a short cut and the distance through the Hole was zero.

Jerry shook his head and said that the idea of folding space was something that was beyond his ability to comprehend. He was amazed by the Door technology, amazed and blown away by the Hole technology and felt like he was a Cro-Magnon man.

Jorge laughed and said that was because he was a throwback. He then opened the door to the communications center and walked in. It was clear to him that he had surprised everyone which was what he had been hoping for. He smiled and asked if anything interesting had happened on their journey so far.

Mia knew who Jorge was but decided to ask who he thought he was to interrupt an important meeting of the very busy leaders of the USS Cosmos Odessey. And what was his definition of interesting? Was being attacked by a missile, was wiping out several million lives, was establishing communications with Dragon and Frog people on his list of interesting things?

Joe smiled and said that the ships devil's advocate, Mia, had self-introduced herself and as she had pointed out so far everything had been rather boring. He went on to say that the most interesting thing was that he had just announced that he was planning to leave and see if he could commandeer another ship, take it, and go someplace that was less boring.

Jorge nodded walked over to Mia and gave her a hug and welcomed her. He then as usual went around hugging and greeting everyone. Afterwards he got serious and said that he had come out to congratulate them on the way they had handled the situation with the intelligent beings that they had discovered. He added that back on Earth more than two hundred specialist that spanned all sciences, languages and a range of other knowledge areas had been moved onto the base.

He went on to say that a special management team had come on board to manage the dynamics of the work that would go on with the beings that they had made contact with.

He would continue to manage the Door and Hole aspects associated with the exploration of the solar system and the universe but setting up relations with the beings on the two planets with intelligent life was now a separate effort that had a different leader and group that would coordinate their efforts with him.

Lydia suggested that they leave the communication center and meet in the huddle room so she could share the latest development that affected the team he had just said he would continue to manage.

Once everyone on the team was sitting in the huddle room, Lydia asked Joe to share what he had proposed to them.

Joe immediately surfaced the desire to commission a second interstellar ship that he was proposing to call Cosmos Voyager. He and the team would go through another Hole to be defined by Tom and Linda and see what they found on their voyage through the Hole.

Jorge nodded and asked where Cosmos Voyager would come from.

Joe said that Doorship Two should be converted and become the USS Cosmos Voyager. The people delivering Doors on Doorship Two would be given the option of becoming the crew for the Cosmos Odessey who would be commanded by Captain Yara Zepfly. The Odessey would stay at her current location for the foreseeable future.

Jorge chuckled and said that he was sure that the President would agree to the request of her favorite Admiral of the Cosmic fleet that would double in size under his command. He went on to add that it was also a request that would give the team a good month of time off.

He looked at Yara shook his head and said that a new Captain would not get a month off. He looked at H^3 and asked what he would be doing if Yara stayed on the Cosmos Odessey.

H^3 smiled and said that he had been promoted to be the Chief Scientific Officer on the Odessey. His only hope was that he would at least make the same salary as a Captain did.

Jorge asked Darian and Samantha what they thought about all the changes that were being proposed.

Darian shook his head and said that things had just gotten back into the normal rhythm that went on around Joe. He was looking forward to the next journey through a Hole but until then he and Samantha would be laying under the apple trees in her parents small apple orchard looking up at the sky enjoying the early autumn weather.

Jorge said that he would act immediately on the suggested changes. He added that he and Jerry were expected for a late dinner back on Earth and it was time that they departed.

Yara smiled and said he should visit more often but figure out how to send out some of the steaks Uncle Ted sent regularly to the base.

Jorge nodded and before he stood up to leave, he said he had one more bit of news. He said that the FBI person that had facilitated the placement of the two saboteurs had been captured and was currently in custody at Lakland. He would be undergoing interrogation that would begin with some special handling by Doug and a couple of his team members when he was on the way to the interrogation room.

Joe laughed and asked if the two biker looking members on Doug's team were the ones that would do the special handling.

Jerry nodded and said that Joe had identified the two.

Lydia said that the two had scared the daylights out of her the first time she had met them. They were as kind as could be but their tattoos on the side of their faces, everywhere on their arms and elsewhere on their bodies was enough to frighten her. Even after working with them, she always had a visual reaction to their looks. She chuckled and said that the only person who still could frighten her more was Doug when he got mad.

Jorge said he would make sure that Doug got his chance to try and frighten the FBI scoundrel. He, Jerry, Doug and the prosecutor, Inés, would be questioning him the next day. He added that the two on the floor saboteurs had fingered their FBI handler in a deal that would allow them to be eligible for parole. He got the groans that he had expected. He smiled and said that they would be eligible after a minimum of thirty years of good behavior that would be served in a maximum security prison.

Samantha shook her head and said even that sounded generous based on the maiming that would have happened if Joe had not insisted that they do a third bomb sweep of the Odessey.

Jorge nodded and said that was the reaction that he and Jerry had but Inés had been instructed by the President to find the mastermind and that was the reason that the two were getting off with what they thought was a very generous deal.

However, he added that the two would be spending the early part of their imprisonment in a high security prison where they would only see the sky for a couple of hours a day.

Joe nodded and suggested that he and the team focus on what they hoped to accomplish on their next journey through the Hole and let Jorge handle the investigation of the sabotage perpetrators. He added that he would make sure that Uncle Ted sent a regular helping of his many versions of the ranch's very delicious steaks while he and Lydia were enjoying their stay at the ranch.

28

<u>The Grizzly Tree</u>

A week later, Joe was notified that the crew of Doorship Two had all eagerly agreed to a transfer to the Cosmos Odessey. He was asked to promote the leader to the rank of Commander and that each of the team members would be given the rank of Lieutenant Commanders. He met with Yara too and the two of them discussed the new members and agreed that they would work well. Joe and Lydia had trained every one of the team members and Yara said that they had all been part of the people that she had also trained with. She added that she was pleased with the fact that they had all been eager to get onboard the Cosmos.

He asked his father and Uncle Ted if he could hold the promotion ceremony at the ranch. He got the approval that he had expected and set the date that it would occur after talking it over with Jorge and Jerry.

Jorge was very agreeable with having the promotion event out on the ranch. He knew that it would be a memorable event and would be accompanied with the best meal a person could dream of. He shared the date with President McAdam who said she would try to make that date.

She let him know that she wanted to enroll Joe in the next Presidential campaign. She wanted her current Vice President, Craig Lebak to become President and as soon as the election was over she wanted to be assigned the role of Interstellar Ambassador to the planets Wŭ and Anura. Jorge said that he was sure that Joe would agree to be a part of the election process.

Jarad had placed the ads in the newspaper as his uncle had directed. He had spent a great deal of time digging into the details of his uncle's arrest and his connection with Mathew Pinkerton III. He found out that both of them were in the same prison. His uncle had never mentioned that fact. He also found out who the people that had fingered Mathew and his uncle were. The most famous one was Joe Elsinger who was some sort of astronaut involved in space travel. He dug into his back ground and found that he had been raised on a ranch outside of the small town of Canadian, Texas.

He took up hiking, fishing, and target practicing. He called himself a hiking baitcaster-sniper, an "HBS" which he then thought Hip-Big-Shot might be a better fit. He started hiking the small streams around the ranch where this Elsinger jerk had grown up. He carried his matte black semi-automatic long range .22 sports rifle hanging on his back in a carrying case.

He had reconnoitered the ranch and found several places where he could lay undetected. The best location was a stand of old windblown weathered oak trees that stood on a high vantage point over a section of land that had the ranch house and barn on the far side.

Aliens We

He was constantly on the lookout for the cowhands that periodically came out to feed the several hundred herd of a mix of cattle. The evening smells of beef being grilled often caused him to want to approach the house to see if he could snag one of the steaks that were being grilled. On those evenings he always ended up eating a can of beans or some soup that was heated in its can over a small open campfire and lamented his plight.

Then one evening he happened to be observing the ranch house when a dark green helicopter flew in from the southwest. He watched as two people exited from the back of the helo. They were greeted by two old men that he took to be their relatives. He watched as all of them walked back into the house. He figured that in the coming few days he would achieve his goal of shooting the two who were primarily responsible for the fact that his uncle was in a maximum security prison.

Joe and Lydia arrived by helicopter the evening after they had returned from the Cosmos Odessey. They and the delivering two helo pilots were greeted and then escorted into the house. The evening dinner was grilled steak, grilled vegetables, and a baked potato. The steak had been marinated in a new sauce that Uncle Ted was trying out. It gave the steak a slight peppery zing that hinted of apple. It was a new taste that Joe figured he would need to get used to. He listened as Lydia commented how appealing the steak's flavor was.

Uncle Ted nodded and said that he preferred his other sauces better and would put a do not use again sign on his new recipe.

One of the pilots said that he would take all the steaks that might have been marinated that Uncle Ted felt like rejecting.

Uncle Ted laughed and said that he would send back each of the pilots with a small cooler that had three different steaks, each marinated in his more popular sauces. He added that he did not share steaks that were of inferior quality.

The second pilot thanked him and said that flying Joe and Lydia home was an assignment that all the pilots always fought over.

The next morning after breakfast Joe asked Lydia if she wanted to practice using their crossbows.

Lydia said that it was a perfect day to do that and when they got back she wanted to take a walk with his father and get caught up on politics and any other gossip that he might have.

Once they were out at the practice range that was used for both their archery and gun firing practices, Joe set up two targets at the far end. The firing range utilized the downward slope that ended at the bank of a small stream. The stream was one of Joe's favorite ones because it had always been the source of the trout that he would catch and then take to Uncle Ted to cook.

He set up the targets and then walked up to where Lydia was sitting on the old dead oak tree trunk that always served as the place where their weapons were arranged.

Joe went to where his compound bow was leaning against the trunk, picked it up and walked to his firing spot. He set his feet perpendicular to the target and relaxed his grip on the bow. He raised his bow arm up slightly and focused on the target and adjusted the angle of the bow up slightly, looked along the arrow to make sure that he had the right elevation and smoothly pulled the trigger.

He watched as the arrow hit the target dead center but just below the bulls eye.

Lydia congratulated him on his first shot and then took her shot that hit the target but was also outside of the bullseye.

Joe chuckled and said that it was good that they had decided to come out because both of them needed the practice. He was just getting ready to take his second shot when suddenly he felt something hit his leg. He dropped his bow and ran to where Lydia was sitting and pushed her backwards over the log.

Lydia had heard a noise but was concentrating on the adjustments on her bow when suddenly Joe pushed her backwards over the log. She heard him say, "shooter" as he pointed to his leg. He grabbed the scarf around her neck and she watched as he wrapped it tightly around his thigh. She was surprised when he took her compound bow, a handful of arrows, told her to stay behind the log and then ran off into the woods as another shot rang out.

Jarad had been laying on the ground in the shadow of the weathered old oak tree watching the house when he saw two people leaving the house. Through his binoculars he saw that it was Joe Elsinger and his wife. He excitedly took his rifle out of the carrying case and loaded it. He got back into position and looked through the scope and watched as Joe took his first shot. He was impressed by the fact that Joe hit almost the center of the target at what he figured was at least a three hundred feet. He watched as his wife took her shot and also hit the target. He figured that the two were experts with their compound bows. He snickered as he patted his rifle and thought to himself that they might have arrows but he had the better weapon.

He looked through the scope as Joe came up for his second shot. He took aim at the center of his chest and pulled the trigger. He was surprised that Joe ran toward his wife and pushed her behind the log. He took aim along the log and waited to see if he could get in another shot.

Suddenly he saw Joe bolting for the forest. He took a shot hoping to hit him. It was clear to him that he had missed. He jumped up and stood behind the oak tree and looked out into the forest hoping to see him approaching. He heard the command to drop his rifle. Instead, he rapidly turned to fire at Joe who had somehow gotten behind him. As he turned he felt and arrow go through his leg. The pain made him drop his rifle.

He was pulling his revolver from his left hip holster when another arrow went through his wrist and pinned his arm to the tree.

Aliens We

He was surprised to see Lydia running toward him with another arrow in the compound bow she was carrying while at the same time he felt a knife at his neck telling him that if he move he was a dead man.

Lydia had watched Joe run into the woods and knew about where he was going. She looked over the log and decided that she would take a more direct route. She jumped over the log grabbed the remaining arrows, picked up Joe's compound bow and ran down toward the creek. Once she reached the creek she ran toward the woods. She knew she was out of sight and would get almost to the woods while out of sight. She then rushed up the bank and came out with her bow held out in front of her. She immediately saw that Joe had shot the shooter through the leg and was approaching him with a drawn knife. She once again marveled at the courage that Joe was demonstrating.

She then saw the shooter taking a gun from his hip holster and without hesitation she shot and pinned the wrist to the tree. She then ran full speed toward the two and heard Joe threatening to kill the shooter if he moved. She took her phone from her pocket and speed dialed Joe's father and told him to send everyone to the old, knurled tree that they called Old Grizzly. She looked toward the house and watched as Trey and Uncle Ted ran out and to the barn. A few moments later the two of them and the four ranch hands all came riding out of the barn with rifles in hand.

Once the six arrived at the tree, Joe hobbled over to a boulder and sat down. He knew he had lost a lot of blood during the run through the forest. Uncle Ted cut open Joe's jeans and was putting on a proper binding over the wound. His father came over and said that he should take his horse and go to the house with Uncle Ted. He told Uncle Ted to call the doctor to come to the ranch and check Joe out.

He looked over to where the four ranch hands had freed the shooter from the tree and suggested they drive the pickup out and take the shooter back to the barn. He told them to wait and let the doctor take the arrows out. They should just park the truck outside of the barn and one of them should stand guard.

Joe rode slowly back to the house and let Uncle Ted help him onto the veranda.

Uncle Joe asked him how he felt.

Joe chuckled and said that what he needed was a lot of tender rare roasted porterhouse steak to make up for his blood loss.

Uncle Ted laughed and declared that Joe would live. He then said that Joe should wait on the porch until the doctor arrived and he prepared the steak.

Trey and Lydia walked slowly back toward the house. He asked how she had managed to get to the same place that Joe had gotten at the same time.

Lydia smiled and said that she had taken the short cut to the tree.

Trey looked over his shoulder to the tree and said that then she had to run in the open all way to the creek. He took her hand and added that she was just about as crazy as his son who went running through the woods and left a trail of blood while doing so.

Lydia nodded and said that yes they were both crazy. Crazy in love and willing to risk everything for each other.

Trey squeezed her hand and said that she was just as crazy as Joe's mother had been.

29

<u>The Connection</u>

Jarad lay in the back of the pickup in agony. The throbbing pain from the arrow in his left wrist seemed to be keeping rhythm with the pain from the arrow sticking through his left thigh and both were throbbing to the rhythm of his heart. He reached up and realized he was bleeding from where the knife had penetrated his neck just below his chin. He suddenly realized how close to dying he had come. "So much for having the advantage of a powerful rifle over bow and arrow," went through his mind as he let out a low moan. He found it hard to concentrate on his current situation. He was suddenly feeling cold.

The cowboy leaning on the tail gate of the old pick up chuckled and said he looked like a porcupine with the arrows sticking through him. He laughed and added that he had picked on the wrong two people. He slowly drawled out that the two had been shot at with missiles, had been the target of a massive bomb attack, had been the target of a heinous sabotage effort, and had escaped from a team of abductors all who either ended up dead or in prison for life. The fact that he had thought to attack them on the ranch just showed everyone how stupid he was.

Jarad shook his head in despair. He was getting cold and he was hungry. He hurt all over and he had to listen to a smart-alecky cowboy who was enjoying taunting him. How could all have happened? How?

Doctor Sink drove down the long driveway to the elegant old red brick ranch house with the green copper roof. The last time he had made the drive had been for Joe's wedding a couple of years back. On this call, he had been told that Joe had been shot and wondered how that would have happened. He was slightly worried but the fact that it had not been an emergency was a relief. He was greeted by Trey as he got out of his pickup with his emergency field kit. He looked back to see the EMT vehicle that also served as the local ambulance coming up the driveway with its horn blaring and lights flashing. He always asked why they drove through the empty country side with their awful blaring noise when there wasn't a soul within miles. He followed Trey up to the porch where Joe was sitting being fed a piece of rare steak that made his mouth water.

He greeted Joe, saw the bloody right pant leg, and knew that the wound was in his right thigh. He had Joe remove the bloody jeans and then examined the wound and asked who had done such a thorough job cleaning it and stopping the bleeding.

After Joe swallowed the bite of steak he had in his mouth he pointed at Uncle Ted and said that not only did he grill a mean steak but he also knew how to cure meat but he said that the wound was just another piece of meat the needed proper tending to.

Dr. Sink laughed and said that he would put a stitch on each side of the bullet hole and then Joe could finish his steak. He pointed at the blood soaked jeans and asked if Joe was feeling light headed.

Joe shook his head and said that he had been drinking lots of water and all the bloody steak Uncle Joe could feed him.

Dr. Sink asked him to stand up slowly and to see how he felt.

Joe stood up and after a few minutes said that he felt fine.

Lydia had been standing by waiting until the right moment and said that she would help him get out of the bloody pants and into a clean pair of jeans.

Joe let Lydia help him get into the pair she had brought out to the porch.

The guard at the back of the pickup was eating a steak that was still sizzling when it had been handed to him. He took a bite and commented that working on the ranch was like working in food heaven. He asked Jarad if he was hungry.

Jarad had skipped breakfast so he could be in position early and the smell of the steak had his stomach grumbling. He knew that cowboy was taunting him. He wished he could throw a brick at him.

Dr. Sink stood up and asked where the second person that needed his attention happened to be.

Joe pointed to the pickup and asked the doctor to wait for a moment while he finished getting into his jeans. He added that he wanted to ask his attacker a few questions before he was whisked away by the EMT's.

Joe asked Uncle Ted to bring a fresh steak and the sides out with him to the pickup. He then zipped up the jeans and then let Lydia help him down the steps. He slowly hobbled over to the pickup. He could feel the pain but it was at a tolerable level.

He stood at the side where the shooter was leaning and asked his name.

Jarad stated his name and was surprised by how friendly Joe happened to be. He heard Joe say that if he answered a few questions he would get to enjoy a steak and the rest of the food on the plate he was holding. The plate then passed under his nose. The grumble of his empty stomach seemed to tell him to answer the questions. He was expecting to answer a couple questions like; why he was shooting at him or who had sent him. He was surprised when he was asked how he was connected to Mathew Pinkerton III. He spurted out that his Uncle was in the same prison as his longtime friend Mathew. He was then expecting a series of more questions but none came.

Joe thanked Jarad for his answer, took a minute to cut the steak into small pieces and then handed him the plate. He then turned and walked back towards the veranda. The answer that he had received had closed the circle for him. Now all he had to do was to figure out how the connection to the sleeper network had been activated.

Dr. Sink had been expecting a long wait as Joe asked questions and he was surprised when Joe only asked one question and then walked away. He climbed into the bed of the pickup to do an initial examination of the wounds. He then asked the two EMT's to move Jarad out of the back of the pickup so he could attend to the wounds.

He figured that he would tend to them before sending him on to the next city that had a holding cell at the hospital. It was clear to him that the wounds were significant but not life threatening. He found that the arrow through the wrist had broken the ulna. He gave that diagnosis to the EMT leader and said that once he was at the hospital the ulna bone should be set and a cast put on the arm.

He was walking back to his pickup when one of the ranch hands said that he had been sent to ask him to stay for lunch. He put his bag into the back of his pick up and followed the hand back into the kitchen entrance to the table where everyone was sitting. Once seated he could not keep himself from asking what Joe had learned from the one answer that he had traded the steak for.

Joe said that Jarad had just solved the case of who had been the person behind a massive sabotage effort that had been perpetrated. That sabotage had been discovered and diffused but who the mastermind behind it all had remained an unknown. That single question had identified the mastermind. What was still left was to fill in a few missing pieces that would complete the puzzle.

Dr. Sink shook his head and said that he had no clue exactly what it all meant but he had been surprised at how quickly the questioning ended. He was sure that Jarad was as surprised as he was.

Joe asked where Jarad was being sent because he would be taken into custody and moved to a location where he could be questioned farther by people who would be asking all the questions that he had not asked.

Dr. Sink gave him the name of hospital where Jarad was being taken.

After an hour long ride Jarad arrived at a hospital that he had never heard of. He was taken into emergency care where he was put under arrest for attempted murder by two military MP's, whose insignia indicated they were Airforce, even before he was seen by the emergency room doctor.

The doctor came in, ordered an x-ray, and then walked away without saying a word. A few minutes later he returned and told the two military personnel that all that was needed was to have the arm put into a cast and the prisoner was good to go.

Jarad was surprised at the speed of his release from the hospital. It was still early afternoon as he was taken to a local airfield, put on a helicopter and then after a couple of hour flight he was escorted to a holding cell and told that he would be given dinner and would be questioned on the following day. The pain in his arm and leg let him know that he was in for a miserable night.

Doug had received the information about Jarad's capture and his connection with Mathew Pinkerton III via his uncle Victor Hurtz. This information was the breakthrough that he, Inés and the two generals had been looking for. He now knew how he and his two men could prepare Lyle Spencer, his FBI stooge for his next day questioning session. They had the top of the ladder and only needed to find out the details how he could have communicated from his cell and activated Lyle and the sleeper network of saboteurs.

Aliens We

Jorge had received a call from Joe and learned the name of the person at the top. He had immediately shared that with Inés and Jerry. It was the breakthrough that they were seeking and now they had the winning hand. He had immediately sent the information to the President. He invited her to another grill out but warned her that this time there was no steak but some great Ahi Tuna that had just arrived from Hawaii via one of his military transport planes.

The President laughed and replied that no steak meant no President.

Inés, he, Jerry, and Doug would be interrogating Lyle the following morning. The conversation he had with Inés was all about how they needed to pressure Lyle to give them the information on who he had communicated with and what his participation of putting the two on the floor saboteurs in place.

Back at the ranch Joe and Lydia were enjoying standing in the walk in shower while letting the hot water, spraying in from all around and from above, soak them. Joe held Lydia and thanked her for keeping him from getting shot a second time. She embraced him and said that she had been afraid that he would kill Jarad so she had really saved him and Joe was just a secondary consideration. That reply got the reaction that she had been hoping for. She let Joe embrace her and at the same time turned the hot water up a notch. She closed her eyes and let the feeling of the hot water envelope her. She knew that they had the soul to soul relationship that she had always dreamt of.

29 The Connection

Joe fell asleep immediately upon hitting the bed but he had placed a call requesting transport to Lakland early the next morning.

30

<u>A Closed Loop</u>

At six in the morning when the alarm went off, Joe let out a groan. His leg wound was now making itself known. He got up and dressed slowly. He got out a black pair of cargo pants that fit him loosely and chose a tooled grey western shirt that Lydia had praised by saying that she was jealous that he had such an amazing shirt. He chose his favorite black belt that featured a black stallion on a carved gold pattern that was a likeness of the tree by the swimming hole.

Lydia saw what Joe was putting on and duplicated his style with the exception that she put on a pair of black jeans. Her belt buckle featured a white stallion on the same gold pattern. It was Joe's present to her. He had both belt buckles especially made for their wedding anniversary.

She asked why he was putting on the look of a rugged cowboy.

Joe smiled and said that he was going to play the crazy cowboy that was going to burst into the questioning session with a hangman's noose to see if it was the right size. He laughed and said that he wasn't sure he would do much good but he wanted to complete the connections between Mathew Pinkerton III and the two heartless women waiting for trial.

He went to the reading room and took down the noose that was displayed over the fireplace where it hung over a sign that said, "Hate hangs in the heart of the heartless."

Joe said that he would arrange for Doug's two biker looking enforcers to take him out of the room saying they would take him to a group that would be ready to help him.

Lydia laughed and said that he seemed to be looking forward to the interaction.

Joe nodded and admitted that he was truly angry about the sabotage because if it had been successful the people that would have been hurt was her and all their close friends.

Lydia could hear the helicopter approaching, she looked to see what time it was only to find out it was only six thirty. She suggested they get down to breakfast and grab a bite to eat before they headed to Lakland.

Uncle Ted was at the stove and asked what everyone wanted.

The helo pilots knocked on the kitchen door and asked if they might get breakfast. The two of them had been the ones that had delivered them to the ranch and had arranged to be the ones to take them back to Lakland.

Tyler, the senior pilot gave a whistle of appreciation when he saw how Joe and Lydia were dressed. He asked if they were going to the rodeo or were actually going to the base.

Joe smiled and said that he was going to be performing when they got to the base and he was dressed for the part.

Lydia laughed and said that as a supporting wife she had dressed to match her husband and had no idea what he was up to, but she would take the whistle to mean that the outfits looked good.

The younger pilot, Veetry nodded and said that Joe looked kind of schmaltzy but her outfit sharpened her beauty.

Joe laughed, handed a cup of coffee to the Veetry and said that he appreciated the complement but flirting with his wife might trigger his crazy side as he picked up the hangman's noose and waved it around in front of him.

Tyler accepted his cup of coffee and said he hoped he could watch what Joe was going to do with a hangman's noose.

Joe nodded and said that he would actually like to see everyone associated and responsible for the placement of all the bombs, that would have killed or maimed his team members, hung.

The Tyler nodded and said that he had heard about the sabotage and hoped the way Joe was planning to handle the situation would help identify everyone involved.

Joe spent his time on the flight to the base talking with Jorge and Doug.

Jorge said that it would be interesting to see what if any difference Joe might make. He said that they were dealing with a seasoned FBI agent who would not be easy to break. He mentioned that Doug and his two biker looking members were going to try to intimidated Lyle during his transport from the base's prison.

Doug's reaction was to laugh and say that he would be ready to make it look like the threat was real. When he hung up he called his team together and said that he wanted to have everyone gather outside of the main office building shouting and holding up signs saying things like hang the Ba s _ _ _ d and a large sign that said "Lynch the traitor and had the drawing of hangman's rope.

He shared the fact that, Less and Jack, the two biker looking team members were going to mistreat the FBI agent during the transport to the interview room.

Then during the interrogation, Joe was going to break into the session with a noose in his hand and threaten to hang the agent. He liked the enthusiastic way his team reacted. He knew that they were all admirers of Joe and Lydia who had won their hearts working with them during the time the Door development was going on.

When they landed, Joe invited both Tyler and Veetry to go to the interrogation viewing room with Lydia to observe his performance.

He went over to the Door transport center and got them to transport him to Doorship Two. He immediately transported back and as he stepped out of the Door receive unit, he looked down at the spot on his thigh and marveled at the fact that there was no scar and the wound was totally healed.

Jorge, Jerry, and Inés walked down the hall to the interrogation room. They had discussed what was about to take place at the beginning of the interrogation.

Inés had shared that she had never participated in such a deceptive approach to an interrogation but she was looking forward to it.

Jorge chuckled and said that neither had he but he was keen on getting a veteran FBI traitor to give them the information they sought and he was willing to try every way possible.

Jerry had said that the fact that the individuals had been placed into the organizations he was responsible for made him angry enough to use every way possible to learn how it was done.

Inés said that so far their very different interrogation approach had worked. She wondered whether it would with a seasoned FBI agent.

Doug, Less, and Jack stood in front of the cell where Lyle was being held.

Less addressed Lyle in a very rude way and said that he should just be shot to save the government the cost of keeping him alive.

Jack grabbed Lyle by the arm and rudely jerked him out of the cell and stated it would be a waste of a bullet. He preferred seeing him hang. He then pushed Lyle against the wall and roughly pulled his arms behind his back and put on handcuffs.

Lyle immediately said they were too tight.

Less reached back to the cuffs and squeezed them and said that he hoped that by the time they got to the room his hands would fall off.

Jack put his hand under Lyle's left armpit and Less did the same under the right hand and together they more or less dragged, pushed pulled and dragged him out to the transport van.

Lyle had hit the wall and door frame several times on the way to the van.

There were several of the team playing demonstrators shouting about tar and feathering and hanging the traitor as Lyle was taken dragged past them.

He asked why demonstrators were allowed on the base.

Doug answered that the demonstrators worked on the base and had decided to make sure he understood how hated he was.

When they arrived at the main office building the demonstrators were even louder and had to be pushed away so Lyle could be taken in.

Lyle commented that he should have been given better protection.

Jack made sure that Lyle hit the door and the wall once they made it in. He apologized but said that Lyle should not try to keep getting away.

Lyle said he was not trying to get away.

Less shouted that he was sorry because he would love to shoot him if he did try as he poked Lyle with the barrel of his gun. It was an empty gun as specified by Doug.

Lyle looked at Doug and asked if it was legal for Less to threaten him with a gun.

Doug said that if Lyle shot him he would be arrested.

Jorge, Jerry and Inés were sitting in the interrogation room when Less and Jack more of less threw Lyle into the room, pushed him face first into the far wall, removed his handcuffs, turned him around and pushed him into the chair that was bolted to the floor and then hand cuffed him to the handles of the chair. They both bent down and cursed Lyle and then walked out of the room with Doug.

The three of them walked around to the viewing room where they joined Lydia and several other observers. It was not a large viewing room and it was a tight fit for everyone.

Inés introduced herself, Jerry and Jorge and said that she hoped that Lyle would answer all her questions truthfully. She made it clear that he was currently facing a death penalty and his cooperation would go a long way in her considering taking the death penalty off the table.

Lyle looked at her and asked how he could be facing a death penalty when as far as he knew no one had been injured or killed.

Jorge said that he had the authority to have him tried as a traitor to the country and that charge carried the death penalty.

Lyle was looking at his purple hands that were slowly regaining some of their normal color. He was a little taken aback at the harsh handling that he had experienced up to this point.

He was surprised by the second general saying that he had been granted the authority to waterboard him if he did not cooperate. The leaders of the country wanted to know how such an extensive sabotage operation could have been set up and he would be quite happy to find out in whatever manner it took.

Lyle was about to object when the door burst open and a person with a hangman's rope rushed in shouting that he was going to make sure that he would never make it back to his holding cell. He watched as his two previous handlers came in and pulled the person with the noose from the room all the while saying they understood and would help him make sure that the bas _ _ _ d never made it back to his cell.

Lyle shook his head and asked why the security at the base was so poor that a mad man could barge into the room.

Jorge said that he was having a hard time controlling his own people who wanted revenge and Lyle was the highest ranking person identified. He admitted that he would need to have a talk with his security people about what had happened. He added that his cooperation would go a long way to reducing the runaway emotions that was currently going through the organization.

"I hope we are getting this all on film," Jorge thought to himself.

Lyle thought about his situation. He knew that there was no way he was going to be set free. He was worried about the fact that the official line was that he was free game as far as interrogation went. It was clear that he was considered expendable.

He was well aware of the unspoken techniques that included injecting hallucinatory drugs and the use of water boarding used to extract information. The angry demonstrators and the crazy cowboy were all indications that the authorities were willing to risk his life to get the information they wanted. The message was clear talk or suffer through whatever it took to get him to talk.

He looked over to the single female that had so far seemed to be in control and asked if the death penalty would be waived if he cooperated.

Inés nodded and said that she would see that he had that in writing and it would be honored as long as he cooperated throughout the investigation and until the end of his trial.

Lyle nodded and said that he would cooperate.

After a moment, Inés asked who had contacted him, how had he been contacted and who had he contacted?

The answer to the who led to a name of a Russian operator.

The answer to how he had been contacted was a call from the Russian operator posing as a cousin.

The answer to who he had contacted led to a person working at the contractor doing the spaceship refurbishing and having him offer the twins a startup role.

Joe had joined everyone in the viewing room where he got congratulated for his performance. He was surprised at the speed with which Inés extracted the information that closed the loop on the case. He looked around the viewing room and thanked everyone for participating in getting Lyle softened up.

The interrogation ended much sooner than anticipated. And as everyone was getting ready to exit the viewing room, Jorge opened the door and announced that he figured he would have too many celebrants to host them at his home so it would be at the officer's club.

Doug let out a Hurrah that everyone repeated.

31

<u>Future Opportunity</u>

Joe monitored the progress of the cases as more participants were identified. The firm where Amanda and Amber had worked for many years was investigated but the owner and all other individuals were cleared of any participation. The owner of the firm had provided some interesting insight when he had shared the fact that he had come to the conclusion that the twins had narcissistic behavior. They worked not for their salaries but for praise and admiration. He had come to the conclusion that the two seemed to have a sense of entitlement. They seldom engaged with the other employees and seemed to regard them as inferior. Joe had not had any close contact with the two and asked the rest of the team if they had noticed the two.

When Jacqueline, the teams psychologist heard what the firms owner had said about the two, she immediately said that the two sounded to her like full narcissists and most likely did not care about the injuries they would cause others. The fact that they did not feel responsible for their actions told her that they were also lacking any empathy which made them not care about the injuries they might inflict.

The person who had made them the offer for a new job had enticed them with an assignment that would make them famous. This person was a senior member of the company doing the redesign of Doorship One as it was converted into the Cosmic Odessey. He was the one that had arranged for the supply of bomblets that were planted throughout the ship. He was arrested and charged with attempted murder and faced the maximum number of charges in his criminal indictment and the death penalty.

The suppliers of the bomblets had been told that they were to be used to make sure top security electronics and other top physical components would never fall into the enemies possession. The people in that organization were all cleared since the devices were approved for such use.

The IT person who had supplied the trigger programming was judged to be innocent of any wrongdoing because his job was developing different triggering codes for the devices.

Neither the bomb makers or the programmer ever had any knowledge of the work being done by Amanda and Amber. They had never met or talked to the two.

The senior member of the redesign company was Lyle's old college friend and had known the objective of the sabotage. He faced the same charges as Lyle but also faced the death penalty.

Joe and Lydia were following the cases but had their minds focused on the future. They both agreed that they would do what they had done when they were kidnapped, they had returned and focused on what was ahead of them.

President McAdams sent them a message saying that Mathew Pinkerton III would see very little sunlight for the foreseeable future and that he had been informed of another failure at trying to get even. She shared that he had a very negative reaction to the failure and was currently under a suicide watch.

She added that Dmitry Ivanov the sleeper contact that initiated the sabotage effort was now the target of the CIA and would be apprehended if he ever left Russia. She added that the CIA was very persistent and would most likely have their man in short order.

He was not surprised that Jarad Hastings, Victor's nephew got life in prison for his attempted murder. He also clarified how he had sent the message that had caused Dmitry to activate the sabotage actions. He was sentenced and sent to the same prison as his uncle and Mathew.

Joe's spent most of his time on the ranch and enjoyed another spring as he waited for the refurbishing of Doorship Two and its recommissioning to be the USS Cosmos Voyager. He spent almost three day a week on the Voyager getting to know every nook and cranny.

He visited the USS Cosmos Odessey several times and was impressed with how Yara had taken command. She had kept her focus on the Odessey and let Lillian take the lead in managing the myriad of people that were communicating with the intelligent life on the two advanced planets.

He was also impressed with Mack Finnegan's approach to learning about the intelligent people that looked to be the human version that had developed on the sixth planet. He was sure that that population would have a very similar but apparently less violent history as compared to Earth.

The crew from Doorship two had welcomed being reassigned to the Odessey and thanked Joe for having arranged for them to have official well-paying officer ranks in his fleet.

Joe let them know that he appreciated the feedback and the fact that they had transitioned so smoothly into their new roles. He added that he was sure they were the right people to populate the solar system with strategically placed Doors.

He, Lydia, Darian, Samantha, Tom, and Linda were focused on the preparation for what they had come to call their Future Opportunity. They visited what was to be the Cosmos Voyager and made several suggestions to bring its transition to higher and more enjoyable standards. They made sure the walkway around the interior was widened, the gym equipment updated, a steam and sauna bath added and the kitchen improved so it would be more hospitable. On the exterior they made sure space was allocated for extra fuel, extra Doors and living units and extra missiles. The improvements were all accepted and acted on.

Tom and Linda had continued to make improvements to the design of the Hole generator and the rockets that would propel the Voyager. They had also reestablished their test center at the base so they could test each of their improvements.

Joe could tell that the two were having success after success when he and Lydia called and talked to them. This gave him confidence that the next transition through a Hole would be successful and as risk-free as could possibly be planned.

He and Lydia were also very actively interviewing additional candidates to add to their next crew. The interviews always included Darian and Samantha. The four of them had grown closer and they had several alternate visits to the ranch and Samantha's home.

At the ranch it was always an occasion for Uncle Ted to try out special meals which they all agreed were treats to be savored.

At Samantha's home it was some special Vietnamese dishes prepared by her mother. Lydia commented that she really enjoyed trying the new dishes that provided a new experience for her.

They all were constantly being asked what their next adventure might be.

They all had the same response that they had no clue where they were going or what they would find when they got there. The only thing they were certain of was that they would embrace whatever they found and grow stronger for it.

The End

About the Author

About the Author

Ronald E. Mueller
remwriter95@gmail.com

Ron grew up in what is now Flint River State Park in Southeast Iowa. The 170-year-old house Ron lived in is built into a hillside. It faces a 125-foot-high cliff towering over the little Flint River. The house and the land talked to him about; the passing of time, the struggle to conquer the land, the struggles people faced and the wonder of nature.

He climbed the cliffs, crawled into the caves, dove from the swimming rock, collected clams from the bottom of the pond, gigged and skinned frogs for their legs. He trapped muskrats for fur, hunted raccoon in the dead of night, and with only a stick hunted rabbits in the dead of winter.

His young life was outdoors, and nature tested him.

He walked to a one room stone schoolhouse uphill both ways. A stern but warm-hearted teacher, Mrs. Henry was instrumental in shaping his character as she shepherded him from the fourth to the eighth grade. A Montessori before its time. It was a wonderful way to grow up.

His experiences inter-twined with snippets of fantasy lend themselves to the adventures he leads the reader through.

About the Author

Characters in the Story

General Jorge		Martinez	General Leading the effort
Jimena		Martinez	Jorge's wife
Lydia	Jade	Tabata	Joe's companion
Joe	Pender	Elsinger	Main character
Jarad		Tabata	Lydia's younger brother
Uncle Ted		Stratford	Like a second father to Joe
Trey		Elsinger	Joe's father
Aaron		Altton	Genius Programmer
Ryan		McComber	Project manager
Harold	Hatfield	Hastly	H^3 cubed key member of Joes Team
Yara		Zepfly	H^3's mate
Lacey		McAdam	US President
Craig		Lebak	Secretary of State then Vice president
Stanley		Black	Science advisor to the President
General Jerald		Delaney	USMC in charge Door transport ships
Doug		Hasterly	Security officer
Linda		Hall	Genius Scientist
Tom		Hall	Genius Scientist
Dr. Radly		Sink	Doctor in Texas
Darian			Second person sent through the door
Samantha			Darian's mate
Piñon Canyon			First hole location.
Colonel Lyle		Sanderson	Piñon Canyon Commander
Jeff		Stanley	Air Force Seargent guard.
Caitlyn		Midin	New FBI agent working with Lyle.
Amber		Trabler	Sleeper Saboteur
Amanda		Trabler	Sleeper Saboteur
Tobias		Mistely	Person owning Flawless Engineering
Lillian		Trundle	Lead linguistic specialist
Bao		Zhao	Chinese linguistic specialist
McMillan		McClain	Mack astronomer
Mia		O'Reilly	Devil's advocate very Irish
Arlo		Finnegan	Irish heritage, Industrial analyst.
Inés		Alamilla	Prosecutor
Cosmos Odyssey			The name Doorship One was changed to
Cosmos Voyager			The second Doorship's new name
Draco (Wǔ)			Fifth planet populated by Dinosaurs
Scorp			Fifth planet leader
Joba			Mate of fifth planet leader
Juss			Linguist on Wu
Anura			Seventh Planet populated by frog like people
Tyler			Older Hilo Pilot
Veetry			Younger Hilo Pilot
Less			Biker looking member of the security team
Jack			Biker looking member of the security team
Fergus	Angus	Barcley	Scottish Linguist
Jacqueline			Psychologist
Mathew		Pinkerton III	Secretary of Defense, president's arch enemy
Jarad		Hastings	Nephew of Victor, friend to Mathew
Victor			Hurtz Friend of Pinkerton
Dmitry		Ivanov	Mathew Pinkerton's Russian base operative
Lyle		Spencer	Mathew Pinkerton's FBI sleeper agent

Published by: Around the World Publishing LLC.

QR Links to
ATWP.US web site